CHASING ELEVEN

By

Dan M. Kalin

FERAL CAT PUBLISHERS
Melbourne, FL USA
2020

Feral Cat
PUBLISHERS

Published by Feral Cat Publishers, Melbourne, FL 32940 USA

www.feralcatpublishers.com

Version 1.0, April 2020

Edited by Sarah M. Kalin, (www.dreamlined.com)

KDP Print ISBN: 978-1970-087116

IngramSpark Print ISBN: 978-1970-087109

ebook ISBN: 978-1970-087093

Contents

FOREWORD

The title and concept for Chasing Eleven is inspired by an iconic scene from the movie Spinal Tap; specifically, a conversation between characters Nigel Tufnel and biographer Marty DiBergi:

> *"..If we need that extra push over the cliff, you know what we do?"*
> *"You put it up to eleven."*
> *"Exactly! It's one louder."*
> *"Why don't you just make ten louder, make ten be the top number and make that a little louder?"*
> *(long pause as Nigel considers the possibility)*
> *"These go to eleven…"*

What does that have to do with a collection of short stories? More than is initially apparent! I've found certain behaviors in myself and others invariably becoming a source of rueful amusement. Generally, this occurs when a person is so focused on a singular obsession they ignore all external indications they may be incorrect and persist in likely folly.

Think of a poker player, betting all-in while drawing to an inside straight. The odds of pulling that one card is very low, but the gambler ignores them, betting everything left, sure this is the one time it will happen. Indie authors are kind of like that: persisting regardless of ample evidence to heaven's vast indifference. Why each writer persists varies by the individual, but is closely tied to the reasons they write in the first place.

As for me, I'm just chasing eleven.

CHARISMA

Simona looked carefully around the garden she had been working all afternoon. *Good! The weeds are almost entirely gone.* Next to her, two small squirrels played while she worked. *They weren't much help today, except perhaps as comic relief.* Simona suspected they were mostly there to make sure she didn't inadvertently uncover their hoard of winter food. The other reason was they liked being close to her when she was outdoors.

"You two are ridiculous. I'm kneeling all day in the hot sun while you play and play." Simona always talked aloud to the many small animals living on or next to her four-acre, wooded property. One of the squirrels shook its tail as if to refute her words before coming next to her leg and placing one paw on her jeans in a tentative fashion. "No, I'm not really angry with you. I suppose you want me to refill your nut dish, hmm?" Their answer was a frenzied tail-up running about, bravely bouncing off of her leg to make the sharp turns.

Simona stood straight up, stretching her back muscles out of the hunched-over posture gardening required. Placing her hands on her lower back she looked straight up at the light blue sky which was now beginning to darken with approaching dusk. Creaking a little, she said a quick prayer to the goddess, before going back into the house. Her cat, Tango, was there to greet her along with Orson the rat. Most people would expect some friction between the normally antagonistic species, but in this case harmony prevailed. Simona expected nothing less, after all. Tango rubbed himself around her legs, while Orson investigated the smells her jeans had picked up from the earth. Moving cautiously, Simona shuffled in to her small but comfortable kitchen and started the tea kettle.

Tango gave an odd vocalization which almost sounded like human speech, ending as always in cat talk with the 'owwweeerrrrr' sound. He was a large, yellow-striped tabby cat, who could easily place his paws atop the countertop when standing on hind legs. Orson was grey-furred and, while big for a rat, was not in the same class as Tango.

"Yes, yes. Dinner will be served shortly. I'm doing it now, see?" Simona prepared their respective food dishes while waiting for the tea water to boil. Soon, Simona was forgotten altogether as her friends feasted.

Tap, tap, tap, insisted a noise from the kitchen window. Outside, a young male crow from her woods stood proudly with a gift: a shiny marble, doubtless lost by a careless child. Simona opened the window and accepted her prize.

"My, this is so beautiful. Thank you, my young friend, it is truly a treasure!" she said and continued praising the young crow. He puffed up and strutted back and forth before allowing her to stroke gently underneath his beak. "I have something for you as well, where did I leave it?" The script was always the same, she would look and look until finally finding a small bag of peanuts. Taking two she offered them up to her young admirer. "Don't eat the shell this time!" Her friend quorked, took one peanut in its left claw and the other in its beak before leaping off of the window sill in flight. Simona watched him for a few seconds smiling, until she heard the teapot announce completion of its task.

Simona sat down at the kitchen table, drinking tea as the sun completed its descent on the horizon. Looking at the calendar, she determined there would be no visible moon tonight, at least not in her little corner of the world. *Good, I'm tired already and don't need to go traipsing in the woods for moon-herbs tonight. I'll log on to my social media and see what family and friends are up to. Maybe a little television after.* Tango lazily swatted at the tea-bag tag, making her scold him half-heartedly. "You keep that up and maybe it will be time for your annual bath quicker than you think, young man!" Tango flicked his tail as if he didn't believe the threat, even for a second. Orson lay stretched out on the table with a full belly, in the final remaining patch of sunlight.

"I'm going to take a long, warm bath before dinner. You two stay in here please, I don't want to share my bathwater tonight!" Neither one bothered to respond.

After her bath, Simona made herself a nice dinner omelet with mushrooms and herbs from the garden. Taking a glass of wine afterwards she sat down at her computer to check on her social media accounts. Ever since her son Ian had set it up she, quite to her surprise, found it to be addictive. Her circle of friends spanned early childhood to more recent, work-related ones. Even relatives she barely knew began to be known online. Sharing pictures and memories had once been a delight for her. Recently, however, a new politician had entered the national scene, dividing friends and family as seldom before. Simona did her best to ignore all of the hyperbole, she didn't care about him one way or the other, but her friends all seemed to be seized by a collective insanity. They either loved or hated him, no matter what issue was being discussed. Worse than that, the divide appeared to approximate halves, so a plurality was never formed. Just two sides endlessly sniping and provoking each other online.

"It's almost like a spell, what's happening, boys," she said addressing Tango and Orson, each of whom had commandeered an arm of her easy chair. "Something like this can be truly evil and set off real wars if it is not addressed early. The amount of power to cast such a spell would be ridiculous, affecting everyone in the world. Even I am affected by it. I dislike the man and I don't even know him." Tango and Orson held their peace on the topic.

Simona threw up her hands finally, "I can't look at this anymore tonight, let's just watch some Discovery Channel, shall we?" The boys were amenable and soon the trio was happily watching a rerun of Shark Week.

***

The next day, Simona decided she should go speak with her coven master, Leopold. If there was a spell affecting everyone in the world, surely he would be aware of the situation. Leopold ran a small shop selling essential oils and fragrances in the arts district. In the last few years, his business had gone from a sleepy concern lucky to see more than a couple of customers a day, to a thriving business. In fact, he employed several coven members as clerks during the weekends when demand was high from tourists.

As it was a weekday, she found Leopold, a grey-bearded man fully owning the look of a prosperous hippie, behind the counter explaining the wonders of essential oils to a potential client. Seeing Simona, he smiled in greeting and nodded her towards the back of the store to a small sitting area stocked with makings for tea. She settled in to wait.

"Thank you for waiting, sister. What brings you to me?" Leopold asked a few minutes later. Usually the only time he saw Simone was at communal worship meetings.

She proceeded to speak of her concerns about the country's new president, which was generating so much strife between people. He nodded as she detailed her suspicions.

"Yes, I believe you're right, there is a spell behind it. I have had to maintain a shielding spell in my store so the effect would not contaminate what we do here. Check it yourself, is the shield working?"

Simona addressed herself internally and found that while she was still aware of her concerns, she no longer felt an irrational dislike for the man. "Yes, the shield works. I was affected by the spell outside, but now it is only an annoyance."

"I initially created it to maintain a calm atmosphere here, but the result is what amounts to a safe psychic space. I need to also treat my residence. Unlike you, however, my effect is that I believe he is doing a good job.

The base spell must be very powerful, as I don't vote red for obvious reasons," Leopold explained.

"Do you have any idea who might have created it in the first place?"

"No, I don't. I did look to see if there was any locus of force centered on the man himself, and there isn't any evidence he is directly responsible. It seems to draw its power directly from those affected, in a feedback loop, so those responsible no longer have to maintain it. There are maybe a thousand of us worldwide who could do something like this, but finding them would not be easy."

"How can we stop it? Should we? I don't think this is an ethical use of power: creating division, sowing hatred," Simona said.

"I agree, but there isn't much we could do to stop it. The spell is now self-powered. It might end when or if someone kills the politician, but it might not if the spell finds a new host. Now, there is an idea! It might be easier to shift the spell onto a more acceptable vessel: to someone who doesn't inspire the same extremes in opinion."

"So the extremes are not generated by the spell itself?"

"I don't think so. This guy inspired the same kind of discord before he became president, but it was on a smaller scale. He was famous before, but people had no trouble ignoring him when they felt like it. I know I didn't give him a second thought."

"How would someone shift the spell? I think it's something which needs doing," Simona asked respectfully.

Leopold looked sharply into Simona's eyes and confirmed her resolve. "I can research it over the weekend, and maybe have something back for you next week. Don't expect formal coven support on something this politically sensitive, though, we have to treat both sides equally. Are you planning or willing to do this alone?"

"Maybe. It disturbs me to see everyone fighting like they are, it cannot be good for our community. Dangerous even. What if he whips up a crowd to come after us again? I know we're in better shape this time around but it would still be an ugly situation. I'll think about it over the weekend and decide once I see what you have for me, it might be something I couldn't even do," Simona said.

"I'll tailor the spell or procedure to what I know of your strengths, which are significant," He said with a quick smile. "Promise you won't just rush into anything before understanding all of the ramifications, please! I like having you with us," Leopold urged.

Surprised Simona colored, "I won't. I have too many responsibilities to casually make such a decision. Why, my animal friends alone will keep me focused on the most important thing: hearth and home."

"Do me a favor, will you? If you come across any comfrey and damiana in your woods, can you harvest some for me? I'm running low."

"Certainly, I was going to ask. There will be a nice moon tonight, so I should be able to find a good selection."

A bell from the front of the shop chimed. "Ah, here comes another customer. I'll take my leave and look forward to seeing you next week, go in blessed peace, sister," Leopold said in benediction.

As Simona walked back to her wooded home, she pondered whether the spell could be transferred to something innocuous, a rabbit perhaps. No, that might be problematic if a predator was to kill the rabbit and the spell escaped to something else. Try as she might, she couldn't think of any one of her friends she would want to burden with what she considered a curse. As she entered her land, the forest creatures gathered as usual in greeting. All wanted to reassure themselves of her health and be loved in return. If you were to survey the health of the resident skunks, possums, armadillos, bobcats, foxes, raccoons, and coyotes it would surprise the uninitiated. In Simona's four acre woods, every creature tolerated every other creature: harmony ruled. Outside in the wide world other rules applied, but having a safe place without parasites, predation, and disease makes a difference.

Simona could sense the stain of national hatred and strife working its way even into her domain, now she was aware of it. That evening, she picked the things Leopold had requested, but also spent time collecting ingredients to create her own shield, similar to what Leopold had deployed in his shop. By the next evening, she had marked the boundaries and invoked the goddess successfully, creating another zone of blessed peacefulness. Once more she was bone-tired, but there were mouths to feed before another bath could be drawn. As she worked to satisfy Tango and Orson, the mobile phone began beeping in an alarm notification.

"I wonder what this is, boys. Let me check," Simona ran over and read the text message. It was a national notification of emergency being declared by the president using the national alert system. The emergency was to announce his decision to contravene the will of the sitting congress by building a wall on the southern border, using emergency powers. Simona threw her phone onto the couch in anger. Moments before, she had felt peaceful and now the cad had reached past her shield to further aggravate. Tango looked ready to vanish if more sudden moves were being contemplated by Simona, and Orson was always ready for a turn in fortune, all rats have that gift.

Noting the alert status of her animal friends, Simona calmed her breathing saying, "I'm sorry to let him upset me, I'll be better now," she said as she went back to making their meal and set two dishes down with a flourish. She then busied herself preparing and packaging herbs for Leopold while her mind raced. Maybe she could transfer the spell to a tree! They were strong, slow of mind, and benign for the most part. It was hard to hate a tree, wasn't it? Unless you were a developer or lumberjack, who would as soon cut a tree down as look at it. No, a tree wouldn't do after all. Even rocks were alive in a sense to someone like Simona, but they too were ruled out for similar reasons.

A long soak in her bath accompanied by a glass of her favorite wine put the final touch on releasing tension. Once more the trio sat down and watched several episodes of a new show about the life and times of the current British Queen. It did its job of distracting Simona from the issue she was determined to remedy. The issue of the American President could wait another day or two.

***

Simona woke the next day filled with determination, somehow in her dreams she had come up with a plan. She decided no one else should bear the burden of the spell if she was not willing to do so herself. It had to be her. As

Simona considered the situation, it seemed obvious a mild-mannered witch who never hurt anyone would defuse the curse. Having made the decision, her life regained the normal rails of its existence. The week passed quickly and, due to the protective field or perhaps her decision, Simona wasn't unduly concerned by outside influences.

Packing up the herb packets for Leopold into her walking bag, she set off once more for his shop. Once she exited the lines of her property, the irrational thoughts poked at her insistently again. The amulet she made as protection for short trips worked, but its power was less than needed for full immunity. Simona gritted her teeth and walked faster. An hour later she entered the store once more and relaxed in the field Leopold had installed. As before, he was occupied with a customer so she made herself a cup of tea as she waited.

"So, sister, do you have my herbs?" Leopold asked with a smile.

"I do, they are right here," Simona said as she pulled the small package out of the bag and handed it to him.

"Thank you! I needed these sooner than I thought. I want to compensate you and won't take no for an answer." Leopold handed Simona a small envelope holding some cash which she tucked into her pocket.

"Good news on another front, I've done the analysis and have a formulation which should work for the task. Here, let's spread it out on the table," the coven master opened a new scroll with the full set of instructions. "As you can see, the shift isn't all that hard, the hard part is that it must be done with the subject within line-of-sight. Have you decided where the curse will be transferred?"

"It's a very difficult decision, Coven Master. Every possibility had issues and I eventually realized the fix might require some personal sacrifice on my part. In the end, I think I should take the curse into myself. I've assumed the fact I am relatively innocuous would help mitigate the worst effects, plus I'm able to work secondary spells to keep it contained."

"Dangerous, Simona. What if the transfer pulls more out of you than anticipated? The President will get something from you in exchange, I doubt you'll be able to choose what goes to him. I'd be very cautious there, what if he gains your powers?"

"I've considered it, and I think it must be done regardless. If he gains my powers, at least he won't know how to properly use them; and he is old enough so there isn't a lifetime left for him to learn. No, I have to do this; he is a threat to our way of life if nothing is done," Simona soberly stated.

"I see your resolve, sister. While I cannot officially endorse what you're about to attempt, I shall pray for its success and your personal safety. Do you have any questions on the formulation?"

"No, the scroll is very logical and straightforward. I'll try to find small ways to minimize the risk, but I think the biggest issue will be finding a way to get within eye distance. The Secret Service will keep me at a distance if they get any indication of ill intent."

"I can help you there, sister. Here's $500; send a donation to his campaign website and ask where or when you can hear him speak. No campaign in the world would ignore the request! I'm concerned enough to support your effort but it has to be our secret! You know the politics of our world," Leopold handed over another small envelope and pressed it into Simona's hands. "If something goes wrong with your workings, depend on me to help set it right. Good luck!"

Her heart warmed from Leopold's support, Simona clasped the envelope to her chest along with the scroll and hurried home to begin the work.

As Leopold predicted, the campaign manager personally responded to Simona's donation submittal and provided a ticket for an upcoming presidential rally, to be held less than 100 miles from her home. Simona gathered all of the ingredients and brewed the potion which would be activated upon recitation of the necessary mystic phrases. The good news was she didn't have to be very close to the President or even make eye contact with the dolt, she merely had to ingest the potion and watch watch him while conjuring. Simple enough. The potion could be ingested before the rally as it was effective for several hours.

In the days prior to the event, Simona acquired some conservative clothing to cover her power tattoos and charms. Nothing must detract from the fiction that her intentions were those of a true supporter of the President. She even purchased campaign buttons and a hat proclaiming her allegiance to the man.

Riding a bus to the campaign rally, Simona noticed the marked stares of those in opposition. Looks of pure hatred and muttered comments about her intelligence were luckily the overt extent of their behavior, probably due to the approximately equal presence of those who vociferously supported the President. *I'm lucky they haven't gone for each other's throats; I'd get caught up in the melee in this outfit,* Simona thought to herself as she averted eyes from both camps.

At the entrance to the hall holding the rally, Simona got in line for the security screening, but first she drank the potion from its small vial and disposed of the glass container. Oddly pleased she had added some sprigs of mint into the elixir, she waited for her turn. A deadly serious Secret Service agent asked for her ticket and ID, which Simona handed over promptly. No one is ever comfortable when going through a security screen, so she didn't worry much about being stiff.

"You've come a long way to see the President," the agent said.

"He wasn't planning to come any closer, so I made a day of it. It isn't that far really, but now I'll have a story to tell my kids," she said thinking of Orson and Tango.

Simona's name didn't set off any flags and she didn't have anything which would pose a security concern, so the agent waved her through, "Enjoy yourself, ma'am."

"Thank you, I will!" Simona managed to respond as she gathered her, now disorganized, bag to her chest and searched for the assigned seating section printed upon her ticket. As expected, it was in a remote section. *Five hundred dollars doesn't go as far as it used to,* she chortled, but it would be sufficient for a clear view of the stage. Above the stage was a gigantic screen which would probably be used to project video of the man himself for those like herself in the very back. *I'll have to be careful to ignore that,* she thought, *the spell wants line of sight to the actual person.*

The venue filled up quickly, and the atmosphere was much like a pep rally in high school. Soon Simona had people on either side of her. The man to her left wore work clothes and the same hat as her. The raucous and sweaty fat woman to her right kept telling everyone around her how the President had changed her life for the better. Simona wondered what her life must have been previously if this was an improvement, but kept it to herself. She was a little bit wary of the man, as he exuded an air of silent menace, although he hadn't done anything to justify the concern.

The rally started with about thirty minutes of local politicians patting themselves on the back for bringing the President to their fair community. The crowd was in a mood to applaud, so they jumped on their cues as directed. The auditorium felt more like a sporting event than anything else. For an introvert like Simona it was all she could do to stay in place and follow everyone else.

The fat woman shouted out the President's campaign slogan, inspiring the crowd around them to chant it over and over in unison. The chant was picked up and spread throughout the large room, along with synchronized stomping of feet. The floor rumbled under the assault, and Simona felt as though she would faint.

The local party leader got the message and started the windup to announce the President. The noise level rose higher and higher, as the crowd felt their power, reveling in the anticipation. The lights dropped, and a single spotlight lit the President as he strode towards the podium waving to his true believers. Simona thought the sound level couldn't increase, but soon found it could. The President was wearing an expensive suit with a strangely long tie covering what must be a very large stomach. He also wore the same hat which was sitting on Simona's head. The fat woman leapt to her feet, screaming her love for the President at the top of her lungs, which were considerable. The silent man was now energized as well, shouting along with the crowd and making arm movements looking something like a salute. The video screen showed a close-up of the great man himself, his hair flying in the breeze provided by the venue air conditioning. He had flung his cap into the crowd, like Elvis, and a fight for the precious relic ensued in the VIP section.

Simona could see the President from where she stood and started the invocation as she stared at the tiny figure on the stage. The overall noise level drowned out the words as soon as they were uttered and if anyone were to be watching Simona it would appear she was another true believer caught up in the rapture of the moment. As the final words were spoken, Simona felt a weight settle in somewhere high in her shoulders, *Nerves, I'm fine. Just fit in until I can get out of this mess.*

Strangely, the crowd began to subside, and the President began to speak. Like many of his speeches, it was calculated to fire up the crowd and included many pauses for applause. Simona knew the spell had worked because the crowd response was desultory at best, with only smattering of applause and none of the whooping and hollering which had greeted his appearance. She sat down and told herself to clap when appropriate.

The President began to notice a difference too, getting more and more animated as he strove to whip up what was previously his crowd. None of it worked, the applause was expected and it was there, but nothing like before. As he closed out his speech, a service dog broke free of his client and rushed the stage towards the President. Clearly wanting to play, the Labrador Retriever rolled over, play-bowed and danced away from the Secret Service agents as they tried to capture it. Finally the President waved them off and approached the dog himself. Immediately the dog rolled over looking up at the President with adoration in its brown eyes. Knowing when he was upstaged, the President bent down and petted the misbehaving pup as it wagged its tail nonstop. The owner was brought up to reclaim his dog, who clearly wanted to stay with the President, but the entire episode brought the most applause from the now-jaded audience. In what was meant to be a big finish, the President waved his arms, shouted his slogans, and ended by running for the stage exit. The dog broke loose once more and ran after him, generating more laughter than cheers or applause.

"Quit hogging the armrest, Bitch!" Sweaty fat woman said viciously to Simona.

Simona started and moving her arm apologized, "I'm sorry, I didn't mean to crowd you."

"Your type never *means* anything, do you? Just think you're better than the rest of us," the sweaty fat woman spat out and punctuated her words with a hard push on Simona's shoulder.

"Leave her alone, you fat cunt!" the silent man broke silence viciously, stepping in front of Simona's seat to address the fat woman's provocation. The fat woman sized up her opposition, including the right fist the man held ready for use, and decided to exit noisily to the right.

"I'm sorry about that, ma'am, but you can't reason with people like her. My name's Gary, and I'll see you safely out of here if you'll allow me to help."

"Thank you, Gary. I must say her reaction came as a shock, it never happens to me. If you can just get me outside, I think I can walk back to the bus station."

As Gary took her arm above the elbow and navigated the crowds, she learned Gary was a HVAC technician and greatly disappointed in the President's speech.

"Don't get me wrong, ma'am, I still support his politics for the most part, but when you see him in person I don't know what all the fuss is about. He's just another lying politician. I thought he was more than that, but glad I came if only to help you."

Simona carefully edited what she told Gary, sticking to generalities on where she lived as well as what her political views actually were. Before long, they were outside the bus station and it was time to part. Gary shyly offered up his business card, swearing he would drive the extra miles without charge if she needed any air conditioning work. Nonplussed, Simona thanked Gary and boarded the bus. Watching out the window she saw Gary standing and waving as the bus left.

On the drive home, Simona came to know Gary and the fat woman were under the influence of the curse which she had claimed. The point was driven home by the evenly split welcoming versus dirty looks from the other bus riders. The good news was Simona was not a proper home for the full power of the curse, engendering fans and detractors who mostly maintained their distance. *Ah well, there was almost certainly going to be a price. My solitary lifestyle can adjust to this situation and I can go mostly go on as before. No more large groups, but I'm fine with that,* Simona thought to herself.

As she walked up the hill to her home, she looked for her friends, but they were nowhere in evidence. Simona unlocked and entered the front door, "Boys, I'm home from the wars. It's time for dinner!"

Normally, Tango and Orson would scramble into the room all over each other, but today there was no scramble of furry paws. She walked into the kitchen, the only evidence of her two friends were empty bowls and a swinging pet door.

Odd! Simona walked outside to her garden, *maybe they are out playing with the squirrels?* Simona called for them, but no response came back. She heard a scrabble on her oak tree and she saw the squirrels sitting on a branch watching her.

"Hello, my friends. Have you two seen Orson and Tango?" Simona asked as she approached the tree. The squirrels watched her closely, retreating higher up the tree as she approached them. "What is wrong with you two?" They didn't answer, and definitely didn't want to get any closer.

At the edge of the garden, there was a bloody rat tail left in the dirt along with a trail of blood headed for the brush at the edge of the clearing. Simona picked up the tail, it looked familiar, and followed the trail. There in the brush, Tango sat eating a large rat which had to have once been Orson.

"Tango, what have you done?" Simona scolded. Clearly, Orson had put up a fight as one of Tango's ears was cut up and tattered.

Tango directed a look of pure, feline hate at Simona, hissed, then retreated further into the brush with his dinner.

Shocked, Simona collapsed onto the recently-tilled soil and cried as if her heart had broken.

***

The President leaned back in his executive office chair, then addressed the Chief of Staff and Press Secretary, both standing sheepishly in front of the Resolute Desk. "What the hell happened out there, Simon? We were going great guns and the whole thing just dried up. Shoot, I even saw empty seats in the last four stops. That shit only happens to Democrats!"

"I don't have an explanation, Mr. President," Chief of Staff Simon said. "Edgar here says the polling took a dive after the service dog incident. Nothing is trending even close to what we saw previously."

"That's right, sir! The tweets aren't being read or complained about and you're losing followers in huge numbers. Right now you're neck-and-neck with the Prime Minister of India, which represents a 30% drop," Edgar read from his notes.

"Edgar, you need to check your attitude at the door. If you can't be loyal, you won't see the six month mark on-the-job. I need can-do people, not excuses," the President chewed.

"With all due respect, Mr. President, this feedback is purely data-driven and loyalty has nothing to do with it. For some reason, people aren't reacting positively or negatively to your activities. No reaction means a loss of trending."

"Look, you useless piece of shit, great data; what the fuck do we do about it?"

"This useless piece of shit resigns, effective immediately. I'll show myself out," Edgar turned and exited the door closest to the President's assistant.

"No one quits on me, you're fired! Not only that, I'm announcing it right now on Twitter, citing lack of competence," the President shouted at Edgar's back.

"Sir, please don't send that, it will only give the press a reason to give Edgar coverage for his side of the story."

"Too late, bitches. I get things done, I don't sit around making excuses. Maybe we'll regain some momentum on the back of it."

Simon sighed and stood ready for the President's next edict.

"What about that other matter? Have the White House exterminators dealt with the rat issue? I had one run over my foot at breakfast, the room was full of them."

"The exterminators have traps out and expect to regain control of the situation very soon. They mentioned it was very strange for the rats to follow wherever you go, it is almost as though they love you."

"I don't love them, spent my whole life in the city and never had a need for any pets. Now it seems every damn cat or dog I see wants to crawl onto my lap. They haven't attacked me yet, but I think it's a security risk. Make sure the Secret Service knows I want an animal-free zone centered on me at all times," the President directed.

"On that, the Head of Detail asked if you would look out the window to see what they are dealing with."

The President of the United States looked out his window onto the lawn. "Goddamnit Simon, it looks like more than a thousand squirrels are out there, all looking at me."

"More than five thousand, according to the Secret Service. As quickly as they are removed, more come in. There are even more birds sitting in the surrounding trees and bushes, it's beginning to be a problem for the landscaping crews."

"Fuck this! Light up the helicopter, I'll head down to Florida and play some golf."

***

The next few days of news coverage were quite unusual: a sitting President being chased off a golf course by resident gators, entire flocks of birds sitting on top of the Presidential golf cart, and many incidents of dogs slipping their leads just to be closer to their Commander in Chief.

OPT OUT

Virginia Sturmkeller, Virgie to her friends, heard a chime ring as her laptop announced a flurry of emails.

Spam, spam, spam, Virgie thought as she looked through the listing. *Wait! Here's something from Quiet Nights Publishing!*

Some months earlier, Virgie had submitted one of her short stories to an open call being held by the publisher. The story was one of her favorites, incorporating science fiction, fantasy, and a solid dose of social justice in the climax. *A very good story!* The publisher had sent a personalized rejection notice promptly, but did mention it ranked as one of the top 150 stories being considered. Virgie wasn't happy being given a ranking either. *What socially conscious publisher gives feedback like that? Are these people cretins?*

Virgie's prior experience flashed through her mind as she opened the email, like irritating grit an oyster cannot shake without further action.

"Dear authors,

We're sending this out to everyone who participated in the recent call-for-submissions. Although we chose other stories this time around, we very much appreciated your submittals. To that end, this email is to inform you that we're running a contest, paying a prize of $100, called ..."

What balls! Virgie said to herself as her temper rose. *This is a fucking marketing letter!* The contest asked participants to solve a puzzle related to the book. While buying a book was not required to enter the contest, doing so would improve her chances significantly. The 80% off coupon didn't change the fact they wanted her to buy the book.

Fuming, Virgie read the email over and over. At the bottom of the email, a small message sat waiting for her: *"To unsubscribe from our emails, reply back OPT OUT."*

"Opt out? You're damn right I want to opt out," she muttered to herself.

Sitting down, she pressed the reply button and considered how best to mangle whoever received her message. She wasn't going to simply state "OPT OUT", oh no! These idiots were going to get an earful. She forcefully typed a reply in one outpouring of elegant disgust.

"Using your author sub list as a mailing list for marketing purposes is a major breach of courtesy. I will not be supporting this anthology or submitting to you in the future. Remove my email from your records, I opt out of anything to do with your firm."

Finding no fault in her work, she decisively pressed send. Over the next few days, she monitored email to see if there was any reply from the doubtlessly chastened publisher, but nothing came and in time she forgot all about it.

***

At Quiet Nights Publishers, Quinton the publishing editor read Virgie's email and wondered at the animus. Every publisher, except some old school bricks-and-mortar firms, leveraged email for any market advantage, as small publishing is always in danger of extinction. Many publishers used such lists to sell their other services to the failed authors. Some even sold the lists to other firms. Quiet Nights didn't quite go that far, but did engage in affinity marketing occasionally.

When Quinton designed the processes for Quiet Nights, he swore they would never charge to read an author's work; they would provide fair author advances with downstream royalties; they would never charge to review an author's work; they would promptly acknowledge receipt of an author's submittal; and they would always provide personalized feedback on rejection notices. The same went for email queries and prompt responses. The only things Quiet Nights sold were books, not services.

Quinton personally managed the opt-out listing himself and fully respected the wishes of all who asked. Something about Virgie's email rankled him, however. She could have just asked to opt out, like several others, but no she had to get on a soap box and preach. *Breach of trust!*

She probably didn't even read the terms under which she submitted the story in the first place, Quinton thought. *It's stated there, along with the clearly worded right to opt-out. Authors who don't read contracts! Good thing there were a hundred stories in front of hers to choose from, I suppose.* Quinton checked the unsubscribe box on Virgie's database entry and placed a copy of her email request into the record as well. *No, it would be unthinkable to not fully honor her request,* he thought as he made a special note to himself. Moving on to his next email, he soon forgot all about Virgie and her breached trust.

***

Seven years later, Virgie was very pleased. Her first "real" novel was being published, according to news just received from her agent. "This calls for a celebration", she said to her cat, Boots. "Chardonnay and catnip, darling!" Getting into her Chevrolet Volt, she headed for the Fresh Foods store. The Volt had seen better days and it was getting harder to repair now that Chevrolet no longer supported the model. But a new car had not been in the cards for a long time.

Virgie's husband had died from a lingering illness just as she finished the final draft. It finally felt as though all of the negative things in her life were on their way out. She had just reclaimed the extra space his life support equipment had taken within their small, two bedroom home in the suburbs of central Los Angeles. The real estate web sites said their house was worth much more now, but without a better source of income there was no way to turn it into ready cash.

Her agent, Estelle, was still pretty vague on how much money was involved, but anything was better than what came in now. She was about to lose her husband's disability payments and her current ebook titles rarely delivered more than $200 in royalties a month. For years, she participated in writers groups and conferences supported by his income, and was known among her peers as an up-and-comer.

Having successfully retrieved the groceries, she toasted herself within the empty space, as Boots played with her catnip treats. *Things are changing now*, she thought.

***

Several days passed without hearing from Estelle. She left voice messages which weren't returned until the phone rang with her agent's tone.

"Estelle! I was beginning to think you weren't planning to return my call," Virgie gently sniped.

"I know, I know. I didn't call earlier because there was an issue with the novel. I wanted to see if I could find another taker before giving you the news," Estelle said in a calming way.

"What do you mean, I thought we sold it already?"

"We had a deal, pending a few prerequisites."

"What prerequisites?" Virgie said as her voice began to rise.

"Due diligence. Almost all publishers now require a deeper dive on unknown or new authors, especially those who have spent time in the Indie publishing space. Cutting to the chase, the Storm Chaser Books imprint of QNI Publishing got back to me and said they had to decline. But, I went on to find.."

"Decline, why? They seemed very interested, and were even talking about film rights," Virgie interrupted.

"If you'll let me finish, I found another imprint, Advent Noetics affiliated with the La Jolla Publishing Group, who signed the deal this morning. They didn't offer as much royalty advance as Storm Chaser, but the back end is almost as good. Storm Chaser wouldn't give me any information on why they declined. I did ask. They only said the due diligence came back negative."

"I wonder if it is because of my online presence? My blog or Twitter feed? I am pretty opinionated there, but it shouldn't be anything objectionable. I'm not racist or sexist, and I support most progressive causes. Is Storm Chaser right-wing?" Virgie asked.

"I don't think so. They paid a lot of money last year for outgoing politician memoirs, most of whom were progressives. Their video division wouldn't be growing as fast as it is if they had an issue there. Virgie, why focus on the people who said no? You still have a deal, it's just with a peer group."

"Yes, but Storm Chaser is hip and growing fast. I wanted to be a part of it. Advent Noetics sounds religious to me, and we both know La Jolla is a pretty staid bunch."

"It's not an option, Virgie. I'm sorry. Look, I'll see if I can learn more about what happened, but I don't expect any change; they were pretty definite when we spoke. Be happy your book found a home, a good home," Estelle soothed.

"You're right. I should count blessings at this point rather than be miffed about the one who got away. Thanks, Estelle! I do appreciate the work you've done and you were right to forego calling me before finding the replacement deal. I would have been hugely stressed and I don't need that." Virgie worked through her disappointment and found indeed that having a deal was ample consolation.

***

Life went on. Now there were book signings and her participation in conferences became that of an honored guest rather than a mere fan. She still felt a tinge of something every time she heard the name Storm Chaser mentioned, but that too faded with time. Her book sold enough to reimburse the expense as well as generate a small profit for the publisher. Virgie herself was able to live frugally off of the royalty stream, although she still drove the Chevrolet Volt.

Advent Noetics proved to be a reliable partner for Virgie, advancing a respectable sum for her next book which also did well enough for all concerned. No one was getting rich, but money was being made. In the meantime, Virgie was getting used to recognition when she made a public appearance.

Midway through writing her fourth book, intended for Advent Noetics, Estelle called with more bad news.

"Virgie, you know the book signing tour we scheduled for the Bookopolis chain? It's been canceled, something to do with their recent acquisition by the QNI Holdings Group," Estelle quickly added.

"I was just getting ready for it! Ninety days and forty-five stores, wasn't it?"

"Yes, but there's more. Part of the reason for the cancellation is they will no longer carry your books in their stores."

"Can they do that? It sounds like discrimination to me. My books are selling alright, why wouldn't they sell them? Maybe we should sue Bookopolis or better yet QNI Holdings Group," Virgie was beginning to get angry.

"I would not recommend it. First, no one has to carry anyone's books unless contractually obligated to do so. We don't have a contract with Bookopolis, so a lawsuit wouldn't go anywhere. Suing QNI Holdings is a bad idea as well. They just purchased several more imprints and book store chains. Don't make enemies when you don't have to do so."

"Estelle, you need to get to the bottom of this. Your client is being singled out for some reason and we don't know why. Start shaking the bushes over there, threaten them if you have to, but get some answers."

The telephone connection was silent for a few seconds, "Virgie, I may have some trouble doing that. I have other clients besides yourself, and two of them just closed multibook deals with QNI Publishing. Another client just had a screenplay picked up by QNI's movie division. I can't jeopardize those deals by pushing too hard on this for you. Look, what would happen if QNI ends up buying La Jolla Publishing? Rumor on the street says they're for sale. If you push QNI hard, they might decide to offload or retire your catalog."

Virgie was beyond blazing mad now. "Estelle, if you can't represent my interests, I'll have to find someone who can. Maybe I should find a new agent!"

Another long silence, "Yes, Virgie, perhaps that would be best. I'll draw up the necessary paperwork and send it over for your signature. I'm sorry I couldn't do more for you," Estelle said as she hung up.

That bitch! Virgie thought. *She wanted to exit our contract. I know my books don't represent life-changing money for her but it was significant enough and dependable. Those other contracts must really be a lot of money. Shit, now I have to find another agent.*

Virgie spent the next week working her rolodex for a new agent. She had met many over the years, but never felt the need to stay in touch with any because Estelle did a fine job. Now she called other authors she knew from conferences and compiled a list of likely candidates. In the usual process of calling busy people and leaving voicemails, it took several weeks before she found Bernard Orstadt. He was just getting started, but seemed competent enough and Virgie would be his biggest client.

One of the recurring questions she ran into during her search was candidates wanting to know why Estelle was no longer on board. Too many of them also had to recuse themselves due to similar ties to QNI, but did convey they found QNI to be a very good party to work with on their other deals. Most were mystified as to why Virgie would be having any trouble there, as there were many authors like Virgie happily engaged with QNI's various groups.

Bernard's first job is going to have to be finding out why QNI has an issue with me, Virgie thought.

Bigger issues were about to derail her plans for Bernard, though. Estelle's information proved to be correct: QNI issued a press release announcing the purchase of the La Jolla Publishers Group in its entirety. Six weeks after closing the acquisition, Bernard was summoned by Advent Noetics for a meeting in San Diego.

Rebecca Mosely, Vice President of Content, was the welcoming committee. "Bernard, I'm glad to meet you in person. I've worked with Estelle and your client for many successful years. Please sit down and let's get right to it."

Bernard declined the offer of a beverage and made himself comfortable, trying not to look at the stunning view of the bay.

"Bernard, as you know, our company was recently acquired by QNI. As part of the integration process, certain directives have been communicated by the parent company and we must comply within 30 days. One directive concerns your client, Virginia Sturmkeller. We have been instructed to sever our business relationship with your client."

Bernard's jaw dropped, "Why? The books are selling well, aren't they? Plus we're still under contract to produce two more. This doesn't make any sense."

"I agree. However it must be done. This doesn't mean we won't honor the exit provisions of the contract. We will. But we have already notified distribution to pull all of the existing copies from the retail and online sales channels. My primary reason to speak with you today is to outline options and ways to ease the transition with your client. As I said earlier, we've worked together well and have no complaints."

"You can't do this to Virgie, the contract…" Bernard sputtered.

Rebecca interjected, "Bernard, you know the contract allows us to do any of it unilaterally, we just have to fairly compensate the author for our decisions. I thought you deserved to know it was happening beforehand. Let's talk options. Very soon, her books will no longer be available on our imprint. You might want to start negotiations with another imprint prior to our formal contract termination, in order to ease the transition. If you play this right, Virgie will make more money than she would have by staying. As part of the termination, we have to pay out for the two books remaining on her contract, as well as a reasonable royalty settlement for early termination. If another party takes on the catalog, she (and you) can get paid twice for the same work. But it takes time to land another deal, so you probably should confer with your client and get to work."

Bernard sat for a few seconds, but could find no flaw in Rebecca's logic. "Rebecca, off the record, do you have any idea why QNI is doing this to Virgie?"

"No idea, but it isn't to save money. We could have waited for a natural contract milestone off-ramp and paid a lot less for the privilege. I'll deny saying this if asked, but the directive came down within two days of QNI taking over. My boss objected and demanded to know why it was mandated; the eventual reply was he didn't need to know and furthermore if he felt strongly about the issue to feel free to tender his resignation. Sometimes you just have to salute, Bernard," Rebecca said ruefully.

Bernard left the office building and drove back to Los Angeles. Along the way he rehearsed how he would give Virgie the news.

Virgie took it about as well as one would expect, with burgeoning anger. The extra money didn't make much of a dent in her fury. Yes, money made it possible to do the things she did, but she was an author first. Virgie valued that title more than anything else, and removing her works from the marketplace was akin to driving a stake into her heart. Bernard gently pointed out the publisher could have withheld releasing her rights. After all, once the privilege had been paid for they didn't have to publish or distribute anything under the signed contract. By releasing her, they allowed her to find another publishing vehicle. The issue wasn't as simple as banning her works.

He also had to talk her down from the ledge when it came to suing. She hadn't been materially damaged and therefore had no case. Even so, Virgie was determined to get to the bottom of why QNI seemed intent on having nothing to do with her. After a bit of internet research, she acquired the name of QNI's General Counsel, Garfield Schuman, and sat down to write him a letter.

Dear Mr. Schuman,

Over the last few years, I have noticed a marked reluctance on QNI's part to do business with me. As QNI has acquired more businesses, my ability to engage in normal business has been significantly affected. I do not understand why my work is being singled out and no one has offered an explanation.

It would be one thing if my work did not meet QNI standards; however, in most cases, interest is shown until a directive comes back from corporate to desist. QNI seems to have no issues with other authors similar to myself, so it isn't a genre or niche issue. Recently, a long-running contract with La Jolla Holdings was terminated-for-convenience without explanation after QNI purchased La Jolla Holdings.

Before I begin to explore options to pursue the matter further, I would prefer to understand the issue from the QNI perspective, if at all possible. I am not typically a confrontational person, but clearly I will have to escalate matters should QNI's future growth impact my own concerns.

Thank you for your consideration and please contact me at your earliest convenience.

Sincerely,

Virginia Sturmkeller

Virgie folded the letter and mailed it the next morning. She didn't expect to hear anything, after all they never explained themselves before, but she had to ask. In the meantime, Bernard was on the job and appeared to be making progress on finding her a new publishing home.

***

Three weeks later, a letter arrived with a QNI corporate return address. The letter was written by a staff assistant to Garfield Schuman, asking to coordinate an informal meeting between her and the General Counsel. Virgie picked up the phone and chose a date for their meeting. They would meet in a Century City law firm, thanks to Mr. Schuman being in Los Angeles that week.

Virgie spent the time thinking about how she should attend the meeting. At first, she considered bringing her own lawyer, but then decided QNI might just clam up at that point. No, it was better to go unattended and see what the hell was going on. Better that QNI should be overconfident. They would learn, soon enough, that Virgie could fight if need be.

The morning of the meeting, Virgie put on her best conference clothes and drove to the meeting location. Entering the designated suite, she checked in with a receptionist wearing clothes more valuable than Virgie's car. Virgie caught the receptionist with a smirk on her face as her eyes did a quick scan of Virgie's offbeat ensemble.

At exactly 10:30, another assistant arrived to escort Virgie into a small conference room, which held precisely one person and a large, official-looking binder.

"Ms. Sturmkeller? I am Garfield Shuman. Before we get started, may I offer any refreshment?" Garfield had a pleasant voice and did not fit the standard template for a Corporate General Counsel. While nominally the same, wearing a very expensive suit, his manner was collegial rather than confrontational.

"Thank you, Mr. Shuman, but no. I'm just very eager to understand our situation and what can be done about it."

"Certainly, please take a seat and I will endeavor to answer your questions."

Virgie settled herself opposite where the binder sat and opened a small notebook.

"Now, how may I help you?" Mr. Shuman inquired.

"I would like to know why QNI has been avoiding doing business with me. As I stated in my letter, if it were as simple as differing standards I could understand it. However, it doesn't appear to relate to something objective," Virgie said.

"Ah, I wondered if you might have forgotten in the course of years, which is why I agreed to meet with you. Ms. Sturmkeller, we are simply honoring your own request; you opted out of doing business with us years ago. Here, do you remember this email?" Mr. Shuman slid a copy of Virgie's "opt-out" email to Quiet Nights Publishing.

Virgie read the email in stunned disbelief, and barely remembered the incident. "This is more than ten years ago, Quiet Nights was a very small, indie publisher with no catalog doing an anthology. How does it have anything to do with QNI?"

"Ah, well, that is a story unto itself. The founder of QNI was a man named Quinton Ellerbee. He started out buying and selling distressed corporations, until he accumulated enough size to operate the ones which could be salvaged. QNI stands for Quiet Night Investments. Quinton was one of those people who liked staying busy and his hobby was reading; so he operated Quiet Nights Publishing as a one-man concern, almost like a toy for him. His day job was running a very large corporation. I guess you made an impact on him, with your email, because you are the only person addressed by this particular corporate policy."

"So because I didn't want him to reject my manuscripts and then send me marketing emails, he is carrying on this vendetta?" Virgie's voice started to rise.

"No. I think it was because you ignored the terms of submittal, which provided an opt-out provision, and decided to preach instead. He wouldn't have called this a vendetta; he always said he was honoring your express instructions. Keep in mind, many other people opted-out without incident or rancor," Mr. Shuman said.

"So, what if I rescind my opt-out, along with making an apology for the tone of my email? Would that square matters? This is so long ago it's ridiculous!"

"Unfortunately, it would no longer be effective in clearing the current state. You see, Quinton felt so strongly about the matter, he wrote a special provision for you into the corporate charter."

"Well, can't he change it? I would be willing to make nice if we can make a new start."

"I'm sorry, I thought it was clear. Quinton Ellerbee has passed, he died more than five years ago. Even were he still alive, it would not be a trivial matter to revise the corporate charter. He could have gotten it done by force of personality, but it would still be difficult. These days, the corporation is listed on the New York Stock Exchange with millions of shareholders. Revision of the corporate charter requires a two-thirds vote to enact. It would cost the corporation millions to even bring the proposal forward."

"Isn't something like this illegal?"

"No, it isn't. Essentially, our position would be that the corporation was honoring your directive and we would litigate the issue rather than settle."

"Then what can be done?" Virgie asked in stunned amazement.

"Shareholders can always propose initiatives for the consideration of other shareholders. I won't say it would be easy to get a two-thirds majority, it won't be. One of the reasons the measure is still there is it would be very difficult to garner sufficient votes to remove it."

"So I would have to buy shares in the firm and campaign for removal of my special provision?"

"It's one idea. Another would be to simply continue doing business as before, knowing this situation exists. After all, you haven't been damaged financially, have you? If we buy another one of your publishers, you can expect similar treatment. Nothing here is actionable," Mr. Shuman stated.

"Couldn't the management team disregard the directive going forward? Changing the corporate charter sounds close to impossible."

"They could, but then they would be vulnerable to being terminated. Most corporate charter guidelines are general, so there is a lot of management flexibility. In your case, however, the instructions are explicit."

"May I see a copy of the provision?" Virgie asked.

"Certainly, it's public information after all."

Virgie read it over carefully and ruefully agreed: the instructions were very direct and clear. "Thank you for the explanation, Mr. Shuman, I really appreciate it. What would you do if you were me?"

Mr. Shuman's eyes twinkled, just a bit, "If it were me, and I was a passable writer, it sounds like a great idea for a preposterous but marketable short story, doesn't it?"

Virgie considered and slowly nodded her head, "Why yes, it does have all of the trappings of a marketable story. Thanks again for your time, Mr. Shuman."

"Garfield, if you please. I look forward to reading it in the near future."

LU'S DEATH RIDE

Allen's phone buzzed with a text message informing him of cousin Diane's death. It waited for him to awaken, intent on starting his day with bad news, even before the morning cup of coffee which transforms one back into a human being. Allen was shocked. Diane was two years older than he, but growing up it had seemed like even less. As adults, they weren't especially close. On the other hand, both always found reasons to sit down and catch up whenever either of them came within range. Allen lived on the East Coast, but had grown up on the West. Diane never left the home turf.

Both cousins were in their early 60s, from a family which reliably managed to live into their 80s. Allen sent a text back to his brother, Simon, asking for details concerning the memorial service. He decided the first order of business was to start the coffee before going back through the scant trail which had led to the announcement.

Reviewing Diane's social media pages, he saw posts for her business had continued as normal, one as recently as the previous day. There was nothing to be concluded from that source of information, though, she could have scheduled the ads months earlier. Her personal pages were completely empty of any reference to illness, although she hadn't posted anything in over a week, which was rare.

Allen knew of a friend of hers, with an online profile, so he ventured over to Samuel's page. *Ah, the mother lode*, Allen thought. From Samuel's page, the details surrounding Diane's death became much more clear. She'd come down sick with something which initially looked like flu and worsened to the point she spent more than 10 days in intensive care before finally succumbing. She'd entered the emergency room with pneumonia and with treatment almost immediately went comatose.

Thinking over the timeline, Allen realized she must have gotten sick on the annual road trip with Auntie Lu, which had concluded just before Diane's admittance into the hospital. Auntie Lu, every year, would gather up a group of relatives to go camping or on a road trip. Generally the trips took less than two weeks, and spanned the entirety of the Western United States. Allen wondered if anyone else from the trip had fallen sick. He still didn't understand why no one had bothered to tell him Diane was in the hospital or sick in the first place. She normally was in regular contact with him via text or social media.

As Allen sat drinking his coffee and wondering what had actually happened, he remembered something else. Several years earlier, Allen and Simon's mother had gone on the trip with Auntie Lu for the first time, without her husband who had died the previous year. On the way home, their mother had collapsed for reasons unknown. When the doctor eventually investigated the potential cause, an aggressive brain tumor was found. The team of doctors struggled to get ahead of the cancer, but it was buried too deep. Allen's mother had died within three months of her return.

Offhand and jokingly, Allen thought he didn't want to be traveling anytime soon with Auntie Lu. Then he remembered another trip years earlier, after which another relative had died prematurely. Maybe the joke wasn't really funny after all.

During the entirety of Allen's life, Auntie Lu's trip had been a big deal. As a child, being one of about 20 first cousins, getting selected to come along was something they had all wanted. It didn't matter where they went, it would still be a large group, and cover upwards of a thousand miles by the time it was over. Usually the travelers were split 50-50 between adults and minor children. Allen thought back on the three times he had ridden along, remembering the explosive laughter which always followed the punch-line of whatever dirty joke Auntie Lu was telling at the time. They would all pile into two rental vans, ten to fifteen people to a van, and hit the road. Typically, there would be two days of travel and motels, three days of camping, and two days to finally return home.

As Allen thought back, there were often episodes of illness on the trip. Some people got car sick and, after a few days, there would always be colds or the flu. There generally were good explanations, such as the fact camping in tents when it rains is not very comfortable. During the camping phase, bathing also wouldn't happen very much and the food itself had the chance to turn on you. Allen refused to eat the mayonnaise after the first couple of days, even when he was a child. But the entire group always had a great time and no-one had ever turned down a chance to go.

When Allen was a child, he never really paid attention to how people were related to him. There were so many relatives, who could keep them all straight? Allen didn't even try. He basically accepted the word of whatever known relative was speaking on the topic. As he thought it over, he couldn't really pin down how Auntie Lu was related to himself. Everyone called her "Auntie Lu" and Allen had always assumed she had to be some far removed cousin or great aunt, since she wasn't the sibling of either of his parents. They had called her "Auntie Lu" themselves when they were alive. Allen wondered why he had never thought about it before, but it hadn't really mattered very much.

Allen waited until the West Coast had time to rise before calling his brother Simon.

"Hey, Simon, Allen here. What's the story on Diane?"

"Hi, Allen. I wondered about it as well. I only found out last night, and thought you would already be asleep so I sent the text."

"I wonder why the relatives didn't say anything. I went online and saw her friends had posted some information during the whole thing, but our relatives didn't say a single word. Normally, those morons are the first to organize a prayer meeting when someone catches a sneeze. I have to say they found a way to lower the bar of my regard for them even more, which I didn't think was possible."

"I don't understand it either. Shoot, I live here in the area and no one even told me she was in a coma. I was told she died, via text message from her phone by one of her kids."

"So there's no information on a funeral or arrangements? I need to know if I have time to get there, takes at least a day of travel," Allen said.

"Nothing was said one way or the other. Maybe you should call Auntie Lu."

"Yeah, I will. About Auntie Lu, how are we related to her again?"

"Huh, I don't really know. I thought she was maybe the sister of our grand-dad. Now I think about it, I don't know where I got the idea. I know she was connected to someone in Mom's family. Maybe we should ask Cousin Barbara, she does all of the genealogy stuff. I never got into it myself. Why are you asking?"

"I never got into the genealogy myself. I'm asking because it struck me as a strange coincidence people die after going on Auntie Lu's road trips. I was joking to myself that we ought to call it 'Auntie Lu's Death Ride'. In all the years I can remember, I can't think of one time Auntie Lu got sick herself," Allen observed.

After a pause while Simon thought it through, "You know, I can't either. You'd think she would have at least had an upset stomach with all the barfing the twins used to do."

"Yeah, the twins still barf too much. Remember when they were both pregnant and had morning sickness together? I don't know, maybe it is all a coincidence and something you get when a widely mixed age group gets together. If there were health problems, maybe the trip just makes it more apparent. Diane was only two years older than me, though, and seemed pretty healthy the last time I saw her."

"Same here, I had dinner with her about a month ago. She had lots of plans for her new business, and didn't mention any health problems at all. Look, I'll see what I can find out here and get back to you with anything new. If you call Auntie Lu, why don't you loop back with me if you learn something."

"I will. Thanks for letting me know as fast as you did - the surprise hit me pretty hard. You just don't expect to lose someone that way, of course it would be bad no matter how it happened. Take care of yourself!"

"You too, and stay off of Auntie Lu's Death Ride!" Simon joked as he hung up the phone.

While he had the phone out, Allen pulled up his cousin Barbara's number and dialed.

"Hi Barbara, it's your cousin Allen. Good morning! First, did you get the news about Diane?"

"Hi Allen, no, I didn't. What's happened?" Barbara asked.

Allen summarized what he knew for Barbara. She was shocked as well. Allen and Barbara had shared several elementary school class years together when they were children as they were the same age.

"The other reason I called was to ask about Auntie Lu. I'm asking because it struck me as a strange coincidence people periodically die after going on Auntie Lu's road trips. I was joking we ought to call it 'Auntie Lu's Death Ride'. Then I realized I didn't remember how she is related to us and decided to ask you, as the family's resident genealogy expert."

"Oh, Allen, that's a terrible joke," Barbara said between laughs, "but I don't know either, which is very strange. Let me get my binder and see. Hmmm, whoa! This is really strange, she isn't in my notes anywhere. My parents had always said she's our aunt, but when I did the family tree I started with the direct connections. I'll have to look further, but so far I am not seeing her listed anywhere. Why didn't I notice it before?"

"Isn't she in some of the old pictures Grandmom had? You've got those, right?" Allen asked.

"Yes, this is really starting to bug me. Damn you, Allen, it is going to drive me crazy until I figure it out!"

"No more than me, Cuz. I might have to just ask her. I can get away with it since everyone knows my knowledge of the family tree is woefully deficient. I'll get back to you with anything I learn. Maybe I'll see you at Diane's funeral?"

"Depends on when it is, I suppose. Tell them they need to do better on letting people know what is going on," Barbara said.

"I'll talk to you soon," Allen said as he hung up.

Time to call Auntie Lu, Allen thought to himself. He dialed once more and waited as the connection rang multiple times.

"Hello?"

"Hi Auntie Lu, it's Allen. Did I catch you at a bad time?"

"No, I always have a few minutes for my favorite nephew. I suppose you're calling about Diane?"

For an old woman, she had a strong youthful voice. "Yes, can you tell me what happened? It just seemed strange she could be in the hospital comatose for more than a week before the news started leaking out. I know I live on the other side of the country, but social media keeps us up to date on Cousin Ed's daily dump for Chrissake."

"I suppose the explanation is everyone thought someone else was telling the extended family. Normally, it would have fallen to your lovely mother, but as we know, she isn't here to do it. I still think about her every day, and the things we were planning to do after your Dad passed. You know I'm not on social media myself," Auntie Lu said.

"Speaking of Mom, it occurred to me, in jest, that historically it's proven fatal for people to attend your road trip."

"Allen, you know I like a joke as much as anyone, but that one is in bad taste," Auntie Lu said with an edge in her voice.

In the past, Auntie Lu had never shown a reluctance to give or receive jokes in bad taste. In fact, she herself had a whole repertoire on nothing more than boogers and poop. In the past, even jokes at her expense rolled off her back as though she were a duck shedding water. Allen wondered at her sensitivity now.

"I don't mean to offend, it just seemed a noteworthy run of bad luck. Diane was pretty young, Mom was as well, and how old was Cousin Bob when he died?"

"He was pretty young as well. We have a large family, with a full range of age groups. The only thing I've come up with, is each person had some health issue no one knew about, and maybe they shouldn't have gone camping with us."

"Refresh my memory, what was Cousin Bob's underlying health issue? I know what Mom's was, what about Diane?"

"Cousin Bob had a faulty heart valve and, if you remember, he never went to the doctor. Shoot, that man didn't even go to the dentist. The yellow color in his teeth was not gold fillings, I can tell you that! As for Diane, we still don't know, but I suspect they'll find she was on an unsafe weight reduction diet. During the trip she had her own liquid diet, and seemed pretty frail to me. She had lost close to twenty pounds and told us she had only ten more to go."

"How many years have you been doing the trip? I know of at least thirty, just from my own experience." Allen asked.

"A long time, Allen, a very long time. In the beginning, the cars weren't nearly as comfortable, and we didn't stop in motels."

"So fifty years? You sure don't seem old enough for that many."

"I can feel every one of those years, nephew. The trip keeps me young, getting to run with kids and adults who I remember as kids. I look forward to it all year long."

"I know, I remember jockeying for position when it came time to choose the roster. I don't think I had any issues myself other than a cold, but Aunt Lu, how many of those trips ended with someone dying?"

"No one ever died on the trip, Allen. Usually, someone gets a cold or the stomach flu during the trip, and the ride back isn't nearly as much fun stopping every few miles for a restroom. Think about it, people cooped up in a car breathing the same air as everyone else. It would a miracle if people didn't come down with something. People never complained about it, though, because the whole trip is just so much fun. When you travel on an aircraft, I'll bet you have the same kind of issues."

"It's definitely true I've caught my share of colds after a plane ride. Auntie Lu, you've been doing this a long time for the family and I never thought to ask you about when you were young. I know we call you Auntie, but I can't remember for the life of me what branch you were in, I think Mom might have told me once, but I have since forgotten."

"I married into the family, with my beloved Edgar. We were never blessed with children, and when he passed young, I started the yearly tradition in memory of him. I know children don't remember things unless they're just interested in genealogy. When you come out for the funeral, I'll get out some of the old boxes of photos, if you're interested."

"I'd like it very much. Speaking of the funeral, do we have any better information on when it is taking place?

"Yes, I do. We're holding the viewing and memorial service at Gadson's this Saturday, and she'll be buried immediately afterwards at Riverview. Diane's church offered up a reception hall and the ladies are providing the food," Auntie Lu said as if she was reading a list.

"OK, thanks, Auntie Lu. I'll have to scramble and get plane tickets. I'll give you a call when I arrive, maybe we can go out to dinner," Allen said.

"That sounds good. Oh, you could stay in one of my guest rooms instead of a hotel, if you want. No one else has claimed one yet. I don't know why I stay here, but it's the house Edgar and I bought when we thought there would be a large family."

"Sounds good, we can go somewhere even nicer for dinner then, since I'm saving on the hotel."

"I'll hold you to it, my boy! I eat like a horse," Auntie Lu chortled.

Allen laughed as he hung up the phone. The odd feelings he had before had faded away after talking to Auntie Lu. It'd be great to put the entire thing to rest after she showed him all of the old papers and photos. He still felt strange and, as many times as he had visited Auntie Lu in the past, no one had ever stayed over in her large, two-story home. When visiting, the kids would run through the house playing the various games children play, but at the end of the day they always went home.

Allen first sent Simon and Barbara an update on the funeral services and timing, then went online to work his way through the airline fare gamesmanship. He had two days to get things together before boarding the plane to Los Angeles.

The days went quickly and, before he knew it, he was sitting in economy class next to a man who sneezed every few minutes of the five-hour flight. Allen couldn't help thinking about his conversation with Auntie Lu and thought it would be ironic if he caught a fatal flu bug on the trip.

Allen's flight landed on-time and he made it to the car rental facility in good time. Now all he had to do was brave Los Angeles traffic to San Bernardino County.

Auntie Lu lived in an old section of Riverside, a town which had seen much more prosperous days, and barely remembered it. She lived in one of the few turn-of-the-20th-century Queen Anne style multistory homes sitting on a one acre lot close to downtown. Allen remembered living in a much smaller place in Bloomington, it had always seemed such a long drive to get to Auntie Lu's, but it had only been a fifteen minute trip on a bad day. Parking on the street, he got his suitcase and walked to the front door. Allen used the old iron clapper to knock. It was exactly the same as when he'd been a child, forty years ago, except now he could actually reach it. The place itself looked older and smaller to Allen, but he could see there was someone doing maintenance. The old lead paint had been painted over at some point, but you could see divots where the old paint had chipped off.

The sound of deliberate footsteps sounded through the door. The door opened and there was Auntie Lu, looking much the same as she had the last time he saw her at his mother's funeral.

"Hi Auntie, I made pretty good time." Allen hugged her briefly and picked up his suitcase.

"I'll say, the traffic just gets worse and worse it seems like. Are you hungry? Barbara and I were just going to sit down for a snack."

"Barbara?" Allen asked in a surprised voice.

"Yes, she's staying in the other guest room. She called after we talked and was asking some of the same questions as you, so I told her to come over as well."

Allen followed Auntie Lu, who was moving as well as he remembered from years ago. "Dang, I can hardly keep up."

"I'm headed to the kitchen table. I always move fast then, like a horse on its way back to the paddock," she quipped.

They entered the kitchen, which wasn't large by modern, open floorplan standards, but had always seemed large to Allen. Barbara was sitting at the kitchen table with a loaded plate. She saw Allen and jumped up to give him a hug.

"Auntie Lu said you were coming. Allen, you're getting old, look at all the grey hair!" Barbara said.

"Here now, I wouldn't be so impolite as to mention artificial means of hair coloration clearly being used by a cousin of mine. The topic of age is just as dangerous for you, my dear, although you're looking well-preserved."

"You're looking fit, too; truce? Auntie Lu has both of us beat in that regard. I don't think she's aged at all in the last twenty years."

"Clean living and a full wine cellar. I'm glad you're not mentioning my hair color, Allen. Speaking of wine, should we open a bottle and toast Diane?" Auntie Lu asked.

"I don't see why not, plenty of time to sober up before dinner. What time should we get there tomorrow?" Allen asked.

"The viewing starts at 9 AM and the memorial service starts at 11. Graveside is 1 PM to give everyone time to get there. Simon said he would drive in from Orange County tomorrow morning. We can get dinner somewhere close by tonight and eat-in tomorrow night," Auntie Lu said.

"When are you going to show me all the genealogy documentation?" Barbara asked.

"I was thinking tomorrow evening after the reception. We'll need something to cheer us up then. I've gotten the boxes out of the attic. They might be a bit dusty, but I'm sure you'll be interested."

"In the attic? They might be completed ruined by now with all the summer heat. I'll bet it gets up to 130 degrees up there in the summer," Allen said.

"It does get pretty hot, although these old homes are better insulated against it. When this house was built they didn't have air conditioning, you know. No, I took a quick look and the records are fine. The pictures are on the old heavy photo paper. I'll bet there isn't an ounce of moisture in the entire lot, so we'll have to be careful around any flames."

Auntie Lu handed full wine glasses to the two cousins and held her own aloft, "To Diane, taken too soon and already sorely missed."

"To Diane," Allen and Barbara said before sipping a small amount.

The three sat drinking wine, talking about Diane, and eating the snacks set on the table for the next hour. Allen's suitcase had been left in the hallway in his rush to the kitchen. When the initial hunger passed, Barbara waved her hand in the direction of the central staircase.

"Allen, I'll show you where you're staying, if you like. Auntie Lu gave me the low-down earlier," Barbara said.

"Yes, that would be helpful, Barbara. I'll tidy up in here," Auntie Lu said over her shoulder as she started picking up spent dishes.

Allen and Barbara walked back out to the entry and up the grand staircase.

54

"Auntie gave me the smaller room because I agreed to come after you did. Yours has a private bath, you bastard!" Barbara said.

Looking back down the stairs, Allen asked softly, "Did you find any old records when looking? She mentioned she had married into the family, Uncle Edgar."

"No, I didn't. I ended up calling her about it, because I feel I must have missed something important, and also because I'm embarrassed she isn't represented. All these years of being there for the family and I didn't have her listed anywhere. Did you say 'Edgar'? I don't think there have been any Edgars in over a 100 years. You don't think she is that old, do you?"

"No. I'm going to wash up and see if I can think clearer afterwards. Is there an ironing board? I need to do my shirt for tomorrow."

"I'll bring it to your room; I did mine earlier."

Allen showered and, since Barbara was true to her word, spent a few minutes getting his clothes ready for the next day. He sent a text message to Simon indicating safe arrival at Auntie Lu's, then went downstairs to rejoin the others.

The kitchen table had been cleared of snack plates, but the balance of the wine was left in their respective glasses.

"Where did you two want to eat tonight?" Allen asked.

"Somewhere expensive - Allen is buying, Barb!" Auntie Lu gleefully stated.

"Why don't we walk over to the Mission Inn? It might be nice to sit outside," Allen suggested.

Barbara and Auntie Lu agreed promptly and, after polishing off the wine, they set off. Riverside had become somewhat seedy in the twenty years since Allen had last walked its streets. In his youth, the neighborhoods leading into the downtown area had an upscale feel to them, and it was safe to walk with a family. Now, like so much of the inland valley, it had become more and more like the worst parts of Los Angeles. Iron bars on every window, iron fences around the lots, and large, angry-looking dogs defending their patch. Allen hadn't thought much of the area when he was young, but now it looked as impoverished as some of the worst places in the world. *Third world lifestyles with first world toys*, he thought.

They came upon a small group of young, Hispanic men sitting on a late-model Chevy, smoking weed, and hanging out together. They saw the trio headed their way, and started the circling motions common to any predator pack confronting prey animals.

"Maybe walking wasn't such a great idea," Allen said.

"Nonsense, I know all the boys around here. We'll be fine," Auntie Lu said.

Sure enough, when the crew got a look at who was coming, their circling became random and less threatening.

"Manny! How many times do I need to tell you to take this kind of stuff out of the neighborhood? Your mother will be very disappointed," Auntie Lu said in a chiding way.

Manny muttered something which sounded like "crazy bruja" and several more conventional Hispanic curse words Allen recognized. Manny and his crew didn't get any closer to the three, almost as though they were afraid of Auntie Lu.

As they walked on, Allen was amazed and said so. Normally, a situation like that wouldn't end well for the gringos.

"Allen, you're underestimating the fear these young men have for their mother. The fact I knew his mother, and how she would react to her friends being poorly treated, is more than enough to change Manny's behavior. Believe me, we weren't worth the trouble with those stakes! About the only thing these cholos respect is their mother. Regardless, it shouldn't ruin our evening."

Allen was able to get a table inside the Mission Inn's open courtyard and they proceeded to enjoy the night out. Stories about times spent with Diane were the main currency of conversation, mixing laughter with sadness.

"Auntie Lu, is there any more information on why Diane succumbed to the flu? I'm still finding it hard to believe she wouldn't be able to survive a cold or flu. Plus, I don't think I'm in much better shape than she was, and I never considered it to be much of a risk," Allen said.

"The only thing which came back was that her internal systems were weak and unable to respond effectively to the virus. She had taken the flu shot several months prior, but this round of the flu was for a different strain variant. The way it was explained to me was the flu symptoms caused a cascade of organ failures, which ultimately proved fatal. The doctors wouldn't take a position on whether her diet and self-medicating had anything to do with it."

"Damn doctors! They are so concerned about their liability exposure, it has gotten very hard to get their honest opinion when things aren't completely obvious. I assume they closed on cause-of-death without needing an autopsy?"

"They sat on releasing the body for a day or so, then finally agreed the case was not unusual enough to merit an invasive investigation. Hon, when people get close to sixty years of age, things go wrong with some people. It's unusual when it happens to someone close to you, but not uncommon in the wider world. Our family has done fairly well when it comes to longevity, but a few will always be exceptions."

"I'll miss Diane. We had a lot of things we planned on doing over the next few years and it won't be the same without her." Allen settled up the bill as the group drank the last drops of their wine and picked up their take-home bundles.

The walk home was completely uneventful. The car where Manny and his crew were gathered had moved on to some other location, presumably taking them with it. The neighborhood was quiet, with no one on the street.

Allen had seen it before, in places like Tijuana further south. The neighborhood becomes a deserted prison for the people living there at night, protected by the safety of strong bars and steel doors. When Allen was young, he remembered an active evening culture with neighbors sitting in their yards or chairs and children safely running rampant in the night. This neighborhood had moved on from those days. In the back of Allen's mind, something was trying to surface. He was trying to remember what disturbed him about Manny's mutterings. The conventional urban Hispanic curse words were not of note, but the word "bruja" caught in his mind. Taking out his mobile phone, he looked up the definition online and found it meant "witch or sorceress". Manny wasn't afraid of his mother, he was afraid of Auntie Lu.

By the time they returned to Auntie Lu's home, it was about an hour before bedtime. The three sat in the kitchen, nibbling on a small dessert produced with a flourish by Auntie Lu.

"Did Manny call you a witch, Auntie Lu? Why would he say that? He had no compunction to also using colorful terms I haven't heard in years thanks to living on the East Coast."

"It's better than being called the b-word which rhymes with it," Auntie Lu chuckled. "Manny has had a tough time since his father died. He has had to support his mom and extended family. Frankly, I don't think he would be able to do so without some illegal activity since he was never the best student. I think I cramp his style a bit, since I'm not frightened of him or his boys. My house has a gothic feel to it, as well: from a different time. Most of the homes were built in the 50s on smaller lots and are single story. I always scare them at Halloween with the decorations and sound effects."

"I'm spent," Barbara said with a yawn and stretch. "What time should I set my alarm for tomorrow morning?"

"I'll have the coffee brewed by 7:30, but we don't have to leave until 9:00. It takes less than thirty minutes to get to the funeral parlor, and I assume you don't want to get there too early," Auntie Lu said.

"No, that sounds right. What's for breakfast?" Barbara asked.

"Chorizo scramble, in honor of Allen's presence. I could go omelet or even pancakes if you prefer." Auntie said.

"No, it sounds good! I haven't had it in a while either. Good night, you two." Barbara kissed Auntie on the cheek and rubbed Allen on the shoulder in passing.

"I'm right behind you, the jet lag is catching up with me. Auntie, I'll help with dishes, give you a clear field tomorrow for the wonders of chorizo," Allen said.

"You're on, big guy! You wash and I'll dry."

The two made short work of the dirty dishes and, with one final wipe of the countertop, Auntie pronounced it done. Allen kissed her on the cheek and headed up to his room.

Allen's dreams were very strange, similar to the time-passing movie trope of showing the world evolving from inert matter to the current date, but punctuated with a cackling Auntie Lu who was the same as she had ever been. He was unable to move, but strangely unafraid. When his world began to spin, like Dorothy caught in the tornado, Auntie Lu rode a flying bicycle laughing and pointing back at him. He woke with a start, thinking he might have had some stomach upset generating bad dreams, but upon reflection decided everything was fine and went back to sleep.

***

The funeral went off without any hitch, the mourners all agreed it was an unexpected but made their own rationalizations on how to deal with those feelings. The religious focused on the wonderful life in heaven Diane was no doubt experiencing at that very moment and professed jealousy. The secular crowd focused on how they would always remember something about her. There were palliative thoughts for everyone's feelings.

Afterwards, at the church hall, the relatives gathered and socialized holding paper plates filled with standard church potluck fare. Allen looked around for a glass of wine, but there wasn't an open bar at the gathering. *Why are none of our relatives Catholic? At least they stock a bar to bolster the spirits of the bereaved,* Allen thought to himself. As things began to wind down, Allen looked for Simon.

"Simon, I think we're about to go back to Auntie Lu's. She is going to show us a bunch of genealogy records and photos of her husband, Edgar, and others. Are you going to join us?" Allen asked.

"No, I have an early workday tomorrow. I'll head straight home in a little bit. Plus, the thought of going through Auntie Lu's records gives me the creeps. I don't know how you can stay there," Simon said.

"Oh, I remember. You always hated going over there when we were kids."

"Something about her home scares me, even to this day. When I was a kid it was all I could do to be polite when Mom drug us over there."

"You used to play just like all the rest of us. Hide and seek: inside and out."

"Yes, I did. If I didn't do something to take my mind off the fear, it would have felt like forever."

"What were you afraid of? The house?"

"I never knew, it just felt like something was going to eat me if I stayed too long. I know it doesn't make a lot of sense, but it persists."

"Some places are like that. I didn't have any problem sleeping there last night, although I remember having some bizarre dreams featuring Auntie Lu. I can't remember the details. I just put it down to having a lot of wine and jetlag," Allen said.

"She does have a good wine cellar," Simon observed. "Enjoy the rest of your stay. Come out again and spend some time on my side of the state, rather than the hollowed-out husk of San Bernardino County."

"I will, and if you ever decide to hit Florida, I have a guest suite with swimming pool access. No one ever heads my way. It would be great to play host for a change." The two shook hands and headed their separate ways.

Allen went off in search of Auntie Lu and Barbara, finding them suffering the attentions of the attending pastor. Allen didn't know what it was, but pastors always homed in like laser-guided missiles to the relatives who weren't professing Christians. Allen suspected the Bible-pounding family contingent of ratting them out, but nothing could ever be proved. Allen caught Auntie Lu's eye and signaled with a raised eyebrow if she wanted to leave. She quickly nodded assent, and turned to the earnest parish-pounder who was attempting to save her soul, in order to make a graceful exit. Barbara latched onto her like a drowning person going down for the third time and escaped as well.

"I don't know about you ladies, but I am sore need of liquid refreshment. What do you say?" Allen asked.

"Our hero!" Auntie Lu said dramatically. "Lead on!"

The trio ran the gauntlet of last-minute goodbyes from earnest relatives, and finally were free to depart. Allen brought the rental car around and they climbed in.

"I thought we were never going to get away from the preacher. I have already blocked his name from my memory, and soon he will be completely forgotten even though the trauma will persist," Barbara said.

"I think he felt a duty to minister to the bereaved. It wasn't meant personally," Allen said and laughed.

"I don't know about you, but as I get older I have a lot less patience for them. How about you, Auntie?" Barbara said.

"If they press too hard, I just tell them I'm a Wiccan or something else which would give them hives. It's fun, I provide details of my midnight nude revels during the solstices. My reward is making their eyes bug out."

"I wish I had the patience to do that! Usually, I just feel like an animal caught in a trap considering chewing my own leg off to escape."

"Well, we're out of there. I'm looking forward to getting comfortable with decent beverages and showing you two my old photo albums."

Barbara brightened at the prospect and chattered on topic with Auntie Lu as Allen drove back to Riverside. Allen looked over at Barbara and noticed she would look older than Auntie Lu soon. He thought of mentioning her health when a chance presented itself, but then sat formulating ways to make the point without upsetting her vanity. Auntie Lu looked technically older, but she exuded a lively energy which overcame the appearance of age. Both Barbara and he were starting to look tired.

Allen pulled into Auntie Lu's driveway and closed the iron gate behind the car. It felt safer to keep the rental car on the grounds, what with Manny and his thugs roaming the neighborhood. They might have a fear of Auntie Lu, but Allen wasn't going to bank on it extending to cover him as well.

The sun was just starting to go down in the western sky, a rare clear-blue sky driving a beautiful sunset. California occasionally would provide a reason why people loved being there, but Allen was glad he was only passing through as a tourist. Looking around the neighborhood before following the women inside, he noticed Manny and his crew working the same patch of roadside as the previous evening. Shaking his head, Allen went inside the house.

Everyone beelined to their bedrooms to change out of formal funeral garb and get cleaned up. Allen put on a pair of shorts and polo shirt before rejoining the other two downstairs. In the living room, Auntie Lu had arranged a group of four cardboard boxes on the table; they looked full of dusty photos and binders. She was running a dust cloth across the boxes in an apparently futile attempt at cleaning. She smiled wryly at Allen and motioned him to open the wine bottle set out on a side table. He opened the bottle and poured three glasses. Barbara and Allen sat down on either side of Auntie Lu on the couch to better see the photos and mementos.

"Barbara, here is a photo of your Mom before one of our trips. Allen, your Dad is there on the right. They must have been eight or nine years old," Auntie Lu said.

"I've never seen this one, look at those smiles! Auntie Lu, you're there on the right?"

"Yes. The man on the left is Albert, son of Henry and Margaret. He used to help take care of the remaining land I had at the time. The year of the photo, he drove the bus we rented for the trip. It was the first year we had something so big, previously we used to form a caravan of passenger cars. We went big for a few years but these days it is easier with a pair of passenger vans."

"Auntie, you look exactly the same except for the hair and clothing styles."

"Thank you, dear! You're too kind. I think I have some more trip photos with your parents as children. Barbara, there is your mom and standing next to her Allen, is your dad." Auntie Lu rummaged around the box, flipping through pictures until she found the right ones. "I liked putting your parents together because they got on so well. It is always a subtext when picking the group each time. Who will be the most harmonious given the overall group composition? I did have to explain to both of them once we didn't live in Appalachia and cousins were off-limits."

"What?" Barbara and Allen asked in unison.

"Just seeing if you're paying attention," she cackled. "It was kind of sweet, they did have a very high regard for each other, but it was mostly innocent at the time. I teased them about kissing cousins once and your dad, Allen, turned red as a beet. Clearly, he had thought about it. He made of point of not being as overtly affectionate with her afterwards."

"No one ever told me anything about that, but then I suppose they wouldn't have. We did visit a lot as children, didn't we, Barbara?" Allen said.

"I do know they loved each other very much, but I didn't have any inkling of anything else. But, my Mom cried for a week after your Dad died. So there must have been something," Barbara said.

"The trips made everyone closer to each other: the shared experiences and all of it. When I would consider whom to bring, I always attempted to pull in parts of the family who weren't as close. After a good trip, they would be right in the middle of the group from then forward. Ah, here we are, a picture of your parents as teenagers." The photo showed a handsome man and a pretty teenage girl wearing clothes from the mid-1950s. "It was the last trip they made before each got married and had their own children."

"Auntie, what happened to Albert? He was in a couple of the photos. He didn't marry, did he?" Barbara asked.

"No, he didn't. Unfortunately, no one knows what really happened to him. One day he went off to take care of some business in the valley and he never returned. It was a big deal when it happened. The police searched everywhere to no avail. We had been having trouble with a local family who were a bit rough, which naturally made them suspects, but no proof of foul play was ever found," Auntie sadly said.

"I remember him being one of the dead-end branches on the genealogy map," Barbara said. "Did he live here with you or somewhere else?"

"He had Allen's bedroom, due to it having a dedicated bathroom. My Edgar was ahead of his time when he contracted for this house. He knew people would want their own bathrooms. Here, let's freshen everyone's glass, Allen. Thanks, dear! There is another bottle on the kitchen counter," she said, "I think there are some construction photos in here somewhere. Ah, here we are! These are some pictures of the ground-breaking for this house. The man standing on the left is my Edgar. We had over 500 acres of orange groves in the valley, and the packing facilities were here in town. You could say oranges and cheap labor built this house," Auntie Lu reminisced.

Barbara looked at Allen over the back of Auntie Lu as she bent over the cardboard box, "Auntie Lu, what year was this? Was your Edgar the son of William and Eleanor?"

"Yes, that was him. He was so handsome when we first met, twenty years after the War Between The States ended. He really could not be ignored by one such as I."

"But, Auntie, he died over a hundred years ago," Barbara said.

"Yes, he did. It was hard being a widow with money in those days, always some man trying to take advantage for love or money. Eventually, it stopped due to my aging and conversion of most of the orange groves to housing tracts. Over time, I had to sell the land piece by piece in order to pay state taxes. It happened to a lot of the old California families with large properties," Auntie Lu said.

"But it makes you over a hundred years old! How is something like that possible?"

"All too easily, I'm afraid. It is hard watching the ones you love die before you, but it is part of the price."

Allen's vision began to blur and his head spun as he tried to stand up, "What was in the drink?" At the corner of his vision he saw Barbara had spilled her drink and appeared to be unconscious. The last thing he saw before losing consciousness was Auntie Lu's face, reflecting regret as well as anticipation.

***

When Allen woke, he couldn't move his arms or legs and determined they were tied. Looking around, he appeared to be lying on the floor of Auntie Lu's basement wine cellar. One of the shelves which appeared to be built in against the cellar wall was actually a doorway to another small space. Panicked, he looked for any sign of Barbara without success.

"Barbara, are you alright? Can you hear me?" Allen whispered.

A sound came from the small bolt hole. Approaching steps, then Auntie Lu, looking somewhat younger than she had just moments before, came forth. "I'm sorry, dear boy. She has already asked her final questions and moved onwards to join the others."

"You killed her?"

"Not all of her. Some continues to live within me."

"But why? She didn't do anything to you, neither of us did," Allen said as tears streamed down his face.

"Not yet, but it's only a matter of time once the questions start. I don't feel badly. You both had every opportunity to walk away from those questions."

"What are you? A witch like Manny said?"

"I'm a lamia, a very old and wise one. Most of us don't last long enough to pass as human, but I've been lucky in my personal habits."

"Isn't a lamia some kind of vampire? But you eat regular food and drink."

"We live on the life force of living creatures, not the blood itself. When we used to drain blood it was because we thought the life resided there, but I learned it wasn't necessary, which is why I alone of my kind have survived. Even the life in plants can be tapped, but it isn't as filling as that of human beings."

"Have you already fed from me? Is that why I am so weak?"

"Yes, but I only took a taste so you could survive to have this conversation. You really are my favorite nephew and you deserve some answers."

"Barbara is dead? Where is she?"

"She lies within the family crypt, over there. You will join her and the rest when your time comes."

"How old are you?"

"Very, my boy, very. I knew Zeus and Hera when they were somewhat less than gods. But these times have been the very best. Family, it is what maintains my interest and connection to the earth."

"So the trips, were just a way for you to feed without causing suspicion?"

"Yes, and for all the other good things which came out of them. The slight taste from everyone is enough to maintain my life and appearance, but not to cause permanent damage to the donors."

"The relatives who died after such trips?"

"Unhappy accidents. My feeding would weaken that which was already precarious, unbeknown to me. I grieve deeply for each and every one. I'll grieve for you and Barbara as well, but life is more important to me than anything which threatens it."

"People know we're here. How will you get away with it?"

"People will know you've left, but no one will know what happened to you and Barbara on the way to the airport. Manny is loading your things into the rental car as we converse."

"Manny and his crew will know. How can you trust him? Why don't you let me go and we forget this ever happened? I promise I'll never be a threat."

"Manny knows what would happen. First to his family and him last of all if he betrayed me. He's no threat. Manny even worships me to some extent. Alas, if only I could believe in your promises. But no, you're too much like my beloved Edgar. You won't let it go, especially now that you know of Barbara's passing."

"You killed Edgar, too?"

"I had to. He learned some of the truth and would not be satisfied with half-answers. He's in there with Barbara."

"Won't the bodies smell when the police come to investigate?"

"Allen, mummies only smell musty. The wine cellar environmental controls take care of the rest. No one will ever know." Auntie Lu bent over to touch his face, immediately his body felt weaker and his failing mind could no longer order his muscles to fight against the bonds restraining him. Auntie Lu bent over and picked him up quite easily. She carried him into the dark space, which he could now see contained many bodies sitting against the walls. Barbara was there, recognized by her hair and clothing, but her body was desiccated to the point of dry wood. He understood now why no one would find the crypt.

"Good bye, my dear. I am so sorry," Auntie Lu bent down and set him next to Barbara before touching him for the very last time.

After a time, Auntie Lu walked back out of the crypt and closed the shelf-door with a final click. To her right was a full length mirror, which she now perused. The reflection was that of a beautiful young woman who could tempt a man before she even smiled.

"No, that won't do. It won't do at all," Auntie Lu said aloud. Staring at the mirror, the reflection slowly changed to a woman of indeterminate age: bright-eyed, substantial, and clearly someone's young grandmother. "Much better!"

She bustled back up the stairs in time to see Manny on his last trip to the car.

"Make sure the car isn't found in one piece, Manny. Don't forget the GPS tracking record."

"Don't worry, Tia - it will vanish," Manny said as he left the house.

Auntie Lu did a quick survey of the guest rooms and found them to her satisfaction. She decided another glass of wine was in order.

Funerals always made her sad.

PIECE OF CAKE

This year Timothy Thompkins didn't wait for his wife, Mabel, to buy a cake he knew he wouldn't like; instead he went out and picked one up himself. You'd think a spouse would know what their partner liked after 23 years, but Mabel would always buy something she liked instead. Tim observed once to friends that she, and her mother, didn't know the difference between fudge and chocolate. Tim, being a man who loved his cake, found this to be a major failing.

The birthday cake was lovely: a large, two-layered white cake covered in vanilla cream icing and topped with fresh fruit. It tasted wonderful, too. While he would have liked to not share, he grudgingly forked over generous pieces to Mabel, along with the dark coffee which Tim made every morning. After several days of cake and coffee, Mabel had had enough and the rest was just for Tim.

Two days later, Tim was down to his very last piece. He sat at his kitchen table overlooking the pool patio, supplied with ample coffee, and savored each delicious bite until it was all gone. Looking around for Mabel, he licked the small plate to gather the last small remnants, disappointing both dogs who were lined up for their cut.

"I'm sorry, girls, this cake was too good to share with you."

Both dogs eyed Tim reproachfully, and signaled he had irretrievably broken their hearts. Tim knew the attitude wouldn't survive through their lunchtime biscuits and paid them little attention.

Pushing his chair back, Tim knew he no longer had any excuse to delay fixing the pole lamp in his front yard. Earlier in the week, just before his birthday in fact, Tim had received a formal notice from the homeowners association pointing out the leaning pole lamp and demanding prompt action to avoid a litany of penalty fees they would soon start to charge. Now Tim could have pointed out the standards said absolutely nothing about the verticality of said lamp, stating merely that each home had to have one and that it had to be functional. Even leaning, the lamp was still functional. But rather than spend time explaining it to the lesser intellects engaged in neighborhood service, Tim decided he would just go ahead and fix it. No point in pissing them off. They could easily find other things for Tim to fix, and being cited for something already on his to-do list was actually to his benefit.

Tim reminded himself that the job would not be as easy as it should have been. The previous homeowners held some strange ideas on the best ways to repair things. Every time something needed to be replaced, Tim could count on new surprises in store. The pole lamp would likely be no exception so Tim mentally prepared himself for coming disaster.

His first plan involved salvaging the existing functional lamp, giving it a fresh coat of paint, and using it upon the new post he had purchased. Three stripped and rusted set screws later, Tim was ordering a new lamp online because the old one had to be cut off of the existing pole. As Tim lifted the now-broken lamp off of the pole, he noticed something odd inside the post. The power wiring attached to the lamp was not alone, there was another run of power line cut off and just sitting there loose.

What the hell is that? Tim asked himself. He couldn't test it for current yet as he would have to remove the pole first, but it was enough to know there was an anomaly which had to be addressed. *Right on schedule for the weird! Well, grab a shovel before I'm sweating so much I can't see through my glasses.*

Tim grabbed said shovel and started the arduous process of removing the grass layer. It involved cutting a circle through the grass and then levering up the sod so it could be removed as intact as possible. Most of the grass would survive assuming the process could be wrapped up in a couple of days. Tim grabbed the oval chunks of sod and placed them under the shade of a tree where the irrigation sprinklers would hit.

Now to dig some sand out of the Florida earth, this should be easy! Tim positioned the shovel and jumped aboard. It went in about an inch and stopped. Tim moved the shovel a few inches and jumped on again. The result was much like the first attempt. *God damn it! I wasn't expecting to hit concrete so soon,* Tim cussed as the sweat built up on the inside of his glasses. The shovel wasn't much use so he got a cardboard sheet to kneel upon, along with a hand gardening trowel. Tim knelt down and started to excavate the dirt. *Home archaeology, god I hate the people who used to own this house.*

After a few minutes, it became apparent the blockage wasn't concrete, at least not immediately; it was tree roots. Big, nasty tree roots - the largest more than 3 inches in diameter. The roots completely surrounded the leaning pole making it impossible to remove without first removing the roots themselves. There hadn't been a tree on that side of Tim's lawn since before they purchased the house five years earlier. Normally when a tree is removed, the service also removes the big roots, unless you paid a stupid cousin to take the tree out. *Hillbilly owners strike once more!* These roots had been left, waiting patiently to be a pain in Tim's natural ass.

After removing enough dirt to expose the roots, Tim took his battery-powered handsaw and tried cutting through them. He started feeling pretty good as the saw quickly eliminated several of the smaller roots, but then he ran into problems with the largest. The saw blade moved slower and slower until the battery was out of power. *Those rechargeable batteries are shit, after a couple of years they don't recharge worth a damn.* Tim had another battery being charged, but he knew it held less than the one he had just discharged in less than five minutes of use. Regardless, he swapped the batteries out, and went back to cutting. Sure enough, four minutes later it was done.

Grumbling, Tim grabbed a hand saw and worked to and fro in small strokes because there was room for little else. Before too long, the roots began to succumb to the revised approach. Now it was only a race between sweaty eyeglasses and the incipient blisters being raised on his sawing hand in spite of the work gloves. By the time it was complete, the hole was 2 feet wide and about 12 inches deep and Tim had built a small stack of roots for garbage pickup at the edge of his driveway. Time to remove the pole.

He dug carefully around the pole to determine where the power cables originated and could only find one, namely the one which had been connected to the light. *Where is the other fricking power line?* Tim wondered. As his hands were at their daily limit for manual labor, he decided to pack it in for the night. Carefully covering the exposed hole and hopefully dead wire leads, he went off in search of a cocktail.

***

The next day armed with a hacksaw, Tim cut the pole in half, so he could get to the bottom of the missing power cable mystery. Sure enough, the cable was there, but instead of exiting properly through the cutout provided this one exited out the bottom of the pole itself. Evidently the pole was resting on the power cable run. *I'm amazed this hasn't been an issue, but if it hasn't maybe the wire isn't connected to anything. I'm still not keen to test it.*

Having the cable exit the bottom of the pole was a problem for a different reason, namely that the previous concrete fill had exited down the inside of the pole encasing the errant power line. *One more thing to fix!*

Tim's neighbor Ed came by to inspect the project progress and gloat. Ed and his wife had purchased their home new, so there were no surprises for them. Not only that, but they had watched three different owners do substandard work on Tim's house.

"Damn, Tim. Those are some seriously big tree roots. Were those from the old oak tree that used to be on the lawn?" Ed asked with a knowing smile.

"I assume so, as there's nothing here with roots like that anymore. I guess the old owners didn't clean up when they removed it. How big was it?"

"It was huge, bigger than my two trees. I remember them running the conduit, told them it was too shallow but they didn't listen."

"What do you think this extra wire is for?" Tim angled the remaining pole so that Ed could see the wire going into the ground.

"You know, it looks like something which would have been done when the home was first built. The builder could have run it that deep without working too hard. I know your predecessors never dug anything that deep."

"Any ideas on what it was for?" Tim asked again.

"It might be the original run. If it had problems they might have decided to just leave it. Or perhaps they intended to install an outlet on the pole and never did. Is it live?" Ed asked.

"Not as far as I can tell. I wondered whether it was on a switch or perhaps a daylight sensor. Hard to tell really, so I'm treating it as if it's live. Told Mabel not to turn on any unknown switches, but she pretty much does what she wants to do so I'm being careful."

Ed laughed again and clapped Tim's shoulder, "Don't worry, I'll look out every so often to make sure you're still standing up and if you're not I'll call the ambulance." Ed walked back to his home, clearly in a fine mood after seeing Tim's predicament.

Finally, Tim settled for cutting the pole out, breaking up the concrete plug with a small sledge hammer. Taking care not to touch anything metal on the mystery line, he was able to pull it up enough to reinsert into the new pole. It was probably the best solution, as cutting and leaving a potentially live wire buried was a recipe for disaster. Better off to simply replicate the situation he had found and shelter the wire unterminated within the pole itself. After that the job was completed without further drama, a new energy-efficient light was installed with a substantial concrete anchor and it should last for a few more years.

Tim sat down at the kitchen counter, drinking a well-earned bottle of IPA, when Mabel came in to shatter his peace.

"Tim, isn't the sprinkler supposed to be running right now? I'm not seeing it and the pump doesn't appear to be on either."

Tim thought it over, "Yeah, it's supposed to be running. If it's not one damned thing, it's another. I'll check into it in a few minutes." He wasn't about to give up his reward for finishing the light pole project.

Mabel bustled around the kitchen, engaging in the Brownian motion women deploy when they want their man to get off his lazy butt, banging cupboards and wiping the countertop underneath his coaster. Tim tried to ignore it, but eventually gave in, swallowing the last of his beer and disposing of the bottle.

"I'll just go and look into the irrigation pump, shall I?" Tim asked.

Mabel acted as though she hadn't heard him, humming a tune as she starting spraying disinfectant across the area Tim had used.

"Fucking cunt," Tim muttered to himself as he walked out of their kitchen into the garage. Why he was still married was a complete mystery. Tim daydreamed pleasantly of a world without Mabel as he walked.

On one side of the garage, the irrigation pump sat stubbornly mute in a puddle of water. In the past, Tim had been able to restart the pump once it cooled down, maybe the "fix" would be just that simple. He opened the timer box and manually engaged the switch: nothing. Peering into the box, Tim noticed the timer clock had stopped several hours prior, which meant either the power breaker had tripped or the box itself had failed. Walking over to the breaker box, he opened the door and read the labels until he found the one for the irrigation pump. Sure enough, the breaker itself had tripped. Moving the switch back to reset it, Tim readied himself for the reset.

Unfortunately, Tim was standing in a puddle of water which the pump had generated. It wasn't obvious, but there was a shorter route to ground which involved a transit of Tim's body. When Tim reset the breaker, the 220 volt current arced through Tim, completing the circuit for a split second before tripping the panel once more.

Tim had time for one last thought before thinking was no longer an option. *Oh well, there's not any more cake left anyway!*

SOCIALLY SECURE

Dave was looking forward to spending a week in California for the first time in several years. His grandmother had held on to life through her 101st birthday, and it was only right to pay tribute to the fact in person.

Dave started life in California but, upon reaching adulthood and the consequential demands of the State of California Franchise Tax Board, he decided to become a tax refugee elsewhere. Over the years, he lived in various states on the eastern seaboard until finally landing in Florida, like many aging consultants. The only disadvantage to living 2500 miles away from the remnants of his extended family was the need to occasionally travel across the country when he wanted to see them. Truth be told, although he liked seeing his family, it was much better having infrequent visits.

So when Gram cut another notch on her yearly belt, it was time for him to render unto Caesar that which was Caesar's. Gram was the last living relative in Dave's direct line older than he. Both of his parents had died in their 70s, prematurely he felt, but the remaining field was pretty empty except for him. There were living younger siblings, but Dave wasn't ready to become the oldest living relative in their family. So a trip was in order, if for nothing more than to encourage the old girl to keep on persisting.

During the last year, Gram had to move from her own home, where she lived alone, to a managed care facility. She'd had one fall too many. The transition had been hard: going from being able to do whatever she wanted in her own time to sharing a room with another resident on an institutional schedule. Still, the adjustment was necessary if she expected to live much longer. The fact she was in a nursing home, however nice and well-managed, contributed to the non-specific guilt and sense of obligation Dave felt.

Gram wasn't able to spend much more than an hour or two in a visit before tiring, which also created a dilemma for a grandson traveling cross-country. By the time he arrived at her door, he would have been traveling over ten hours, combining the flight and drive from the airport. It didn't make sense economically, to make the effort solely for a single two-hour visit. He thought the situation over and came up with a solution. He would center his travels around where Gram lived and see her every other day for a week. The extra day would provide a chance for her to rest, and give him the opportunity to recount stories of his travels about the state on the off-day.

Dave had relatives both north and south so it shouldn't be too hard to arrange visits. In fact, in recent years Dave had reestablished contact with one of his cousins, Becky Saunders, on social media. She and her brother, Steve, were witty participants in the everyday social media whirl of relatives. Many were the times something Becky or Steve posted brought a huge smile to Dave's face.

Thinking back, Dave realized the last time he had actually seen Becky was during his high school years. Try as he might, he couldn't remember ever meeting the older brother Steve. He must have done so, as Dave and Becky were classmates in third grade, but Steve simply wasn't there in memory. Steve's online sense of humor was wry, witty, and subversive – exactly what Dave enjoyed in others. Becky's humor was similar, and the two siblings each used the other as a foil when making their posts. They lived together in Sacramento since Steve's health was occasionally suspect and he needed help.

Dave's remembered Becky as the beautiful, smart cousin who seemed more cultured than her farm-raised, country cousins. She even took violin lessons, rather than the normal band instruments more common to Dave's family. In addition, Becky's mom always served ice cream when the get-togethers were at her home, which was a huge point-getter in Dave's childhood rankings.

It would be fun to see her once more. After all, it had been more than 45 years and wasn't likely Dave would have another chance any time soon. He planned to take them out to lunch and provide the ice cream this time.

Accounting for the difference in time zones, Dave sent an email to Becky asking if she and Steve would be available for lunch on Thursday of his travel week. He didn't expect any issues, if they were actually there, the normal Saunders family answer to such a request was always expected to be an enthusiastic "Yes!" Dave spent the next several days planning for hotels and sufficient lead time to drive from one place to the other, before he realized he hadn't heard from Becky.

Checking his social media page, he saw she had been online within the last 8 hours. Perhaps she didn't get his email, sometimes Dave's emails would be relegated to spam folders due to his dodgy, but reasonably-priced, server provider. So Dave sent a quick text message using the social media platform.

"Hi Becky, I sent an email which you might not have gotten regarding a trip I'm planning to your area. I wanted to see if you and Steve were available on Thursday for lunch so we can all catch up. Let me know and I'll make plans accordingly. Love, Dave."

There, he thought, *that should get through without any hiccups!*

After several hours, Becky made a cryptic response. "Dave, I got the email. I was planning to respond but things got away from me. I'll send something by tomorrow. Love, Becky."

What the hell is this? It was a very strange response to his request, if Becky and Steve weren't available he'd be disappointed but he would understand. People are busy and have their own lives.

Dave kept an eye out for Becky's reply the next day and ran to read it when it arrived.

"Davey, how wonderful you get to come to California to visit. I didn't answer you right away because I have been trying to decide how to phrase my answer. The short version is, I don't know. The long version is much more complicated. Two things I don't seriously discuss on social media: Steve's physical health and my mental health. Steve has serious bouts with diverticulitis and back problems. That is part of my reason for living here with him. My own

problems are the rest of the reason I live with him. I have had several nervous breakdowns/suicide attempts in my lifetime. I have a severe anxiety disorder that makes social life painful at best, panic-ridden at worst.

Don't get me wrong. I would love to see you, but I know that I might also back out at the last minute. I tend to overthink and frighten myself into a "tharn" state of mind. (Watership Down reference)

So, can I think about it and get back to you?

With gratitude for your understanding, your loving and crazy cousin, Becky"

Dumbfounded, Dave read the email. In some ways, he had known about some of Becky's previous issues; but, in the way of large, inclusive families, the actual details had always been of secondary import. One of her sisters had taken her own life, years ago, but Dave hadn't known her all that well. As he sat thinking about it, he realized he didn't know Becky very well either. After some additional thought, he sat down and wrote out a reply.

"No worries. Actually, I was coming to that area mostly to see you and Steve. Don't feel pressured by it, however. It's just the result of me making a list of people I want to visit before I cash in my chips. I'm not being morbid, no known ailments to speak of, just reflective. It occurred to me a while back that I hadn't seen you in more than 40 years. I enjoy interacting with you two online and wanted to do so live. I don't really remember Steve from childhood, so with him it would be filling in blanks. I have other relatives in Redwood City, too.

I laughed when you said tharn, I knew exactly what it was without a reference. I've had it on occasion myself (which really plays havoc when you need to interact on business): going tharn. Lost some great girlfriends in the day when they saw it. It doesn't happen often anymore, I don't surprise as easily, but the over-thinking aspect of it does. My brain never stops scenario analysis, ever. But I try to take more risks these days, not for the sake of it, but because it doesn't matter as much.

I'll play it by ear, I'm getting a rental car with unlimited mileage so could easily be there. Thank you for sharing the below, I didn't know the back-story, it must have been hard to relate.

I'll keep you updated on when I'll be in the area, and leave it to you. I'll understand either way, because it could easily have been me.

Love, Dave"

There, he thought to himself, *I'll reach out once more when it is closer to the date and see what comes of it.* Dave did have other things he could do in the area, and he thought being there might provide enough pressure to break through any block Becky might be having. Getting a big hug from a long-lost relative didn't have to be a stressful experience, did it?

The other arrangements proved to be much easier to settle, as the other relatives were more than happy to open their schedules to accommodate a visit. The challenge was going to be doing all the driving. Gram lived in Santa Maria, California which was located close to the coast midway between Los Angeles and San Francisco. Dave planned to fly into Los Angeles and immediately make the drive to Santa Maria, staying in a nearby hotel. The next day, he would spend quality time with Gram and then drive north towards Sacramento. He didn't plan to go the whole distance, just far enough to where the next morning's drive would be reasonable and then arrive in Sacramento before lunch.

Dave tried to put the whole episode with Becky out of his mind for the next few weeks as there was little point in over-thinking it. However, the unsettled gap in his trip schedule kept returning to nag at his peace of mind. Several days before the trip, he reached out once more.

"Here we go, my promised update. I still plan to head up your way for the day Thursday. Let me know if you and/or Steve feel up to a free lunch. I'm going to be there regardless; at a minimum I will visit the Sacramento area murder scenes from my new book, take some pictures, etc. I'm thinking it will add some oomph or human interest to the website marketing.

Call or send me a text on the day of or before, and we'll take it from there.

I would love to see you, but no pressure!
Love, Dave"

Several hours passed before his computer chimed notification of a new email. Becky's response was brief.

"At this point, unlikely. Steve has had a bad diverticulitis episode. He is still pretty weak. Where are your murder sites? I hope they are fictional."

Dave had written a long-winded thriller which was set in the twenty largest metropolitan areas in the United States, one of the murders occurred in Sacramento purely by coincidence. Dave used online satellite imagery to identify local geographical details for use in his story. He felt describing an existing place would add an extra level of interest for the book. After all, it always worked for him as a reader. He was planning to take a number of photos to use for the website promotional text, and if Becky truly didn't want to be seen, he could find other things to do while he was there.

At no time, however, did he consider calling off that portion of his itinerary. Becky might change her mind if she knew he was already there. One great thing about social media was the ability to check in with location information. Maybe he could post a picture of an eatery close to where they lived. Dave had their address because he had sent a copy of his previous book to them before. Becky wrote excellent, thoughtful reviews and Indie authors value those highly.

Setting the issue aside, Dave turned his attention to the logistics of making the trip. Two days later, he was on a morning flight to Los Angeles. The best thing about travelling west was the travel direction worked with the time zones to render a two hour differential. He arrived in the morning in spite of the five-hour flight. The rental car pickup went well and an hour after Dave landed he was stuck in LA traffic on the road to Santa Maria. As always, he needed to make the adjustment from the relatively relaxed driving style of a Florida beach town to the high-pressure environment of Southern California. It was a paradox that Dave felt safer in the high-pressure setting which boasted better drivers, than the one with slow retirees driving late-model land-whale vehicles. In Florida, you weren't sure the driver behind you was going to stop until they actually did so.

The three-hour drive went by quickly, moving up the scenic coast from Los Angeles to Santa Barbara, turning inland for several miles at Gaviota Beach into the gem of a valley which held Santa Maria. Dave wasn't scheduled to call upon his Gram until the next morning, but he drove by the facility to get an idea of how to best arrive. Then he went to the hotel in time for the happy hour free drink special.

The next day came quickly and morning went fully as expected. The extra care of the previous day paid off when Dave checked Gram out for lunch at her favorite local restaurant. He parked the car next to a facility exit and helped her traverse the last few feet to the passenger door. Gram couldn't move without a standup walker, but she was motivated to get to her restaurant. Gram had been going to the same restaurant for over twenty years, the staff knew her very well and always made a big fuss when she was able to come in.

"So, Davey, what are your plans for the next few days?" she asked after being seated.

Dave quickly ran through his itinerary, paying special attention to the time he would be spending with her. He talked a little about cousin Becky and how odd a situation he found it to be. The Saunders branch of the family had ever been known as welcoming and non-judgmental. Becky's responses just didn't compute.

"You're still planning to go up there, right?" Gram asked.

"Yes, I have some pictures to take and she still might change her mind. If she's suicidal or depressed I don't want to put any more pressure on her, so I thought I would just make it clear I was there."

"Yes, but that approach only makes sense to someone who isn't depressed, Dave. If she's deep into it, she probably has a hard time finding the energy to use the restroom, let alone getting gussied up to meet someone she hasn't seen in forty years. Does she have any recent pictures of you?"

"Yes, I put up a few on social media. She has posted a few as well, meeting with other relatives I might add."

"How well has she aged, Dave?"

"Not too bad. I would recognize her on the street, she looks a lot like her older sister and mother used to when I was young. She's put on weight and isn't the slender, long-haired flower child she was in her youth, but shoot, I'm not the captain of the swim team anymore either!"

"Yes, but as these things go, you still look pretty good for your age group, don't you?"

"I'm not happy about the lack of hair or the extra ten pounds, but I don't feel too bad about it."

"I know a little bit about depression, Dave. If she feels her looks have suffered and is depressed on top of it, she might want to be a shut-in and not see anyone," Gram stated. "Fetch me some more salsa, would you?"

"Sure, here you go," Dave said as he handed the small bowls across the table. "Gram, I don't care what she looks like, none of that would stop me from giving her a big hug when I see her. Plus, she's helped me a lot with her reviews of my books. I also admit to feeling bad I don't remember

Steve at all, I hoped to get to the bottom of it when I met him. My memory has been so good for so many years it is hard to accept I might simply have forgotten him."

"First, this isn't about you, Dave. It's how comfortable she is seeing you after all these years," Gram waved her fork in emphasis. "You might want to consider simply dropping by. Don't give her time to stress or think too much about it. Bring a present, chocolates are usually best, everyone likes chocolates! Once you're there, she'll see it really wasn't something to worry about, but leaving it to her to think about on her own might not get her off the dime."

"I hate popping-in on people, I tried it once or twice in my youth and decided it wasn't for me."

"If you really want to see her, you're going to have to make an exception. Think about it, you're going to be there anyway. Now, what should I get for dessert?" Gram brushed the crumbs off the front of her sweater and turned to the menu with relish, even though she knew it all by heart.

True to expectation, Gram ran out of energy after visiting two hours, and getting back to her shared room took the last of it. She was able to use her walker without any incidents, which was amazing in itself for someone 101 years old. Dave signed her back in with the residence staff and, as he passed her room on the way out, he saw she was already preparing to take a nap. With a smile, he left a small box of chocolates with the staff to place on her nightstand as a waking surprise. Everyone likes chocolates.

Getting back into his trusty rental car, Dave set course for a hotel in Los Banos. On the long drive, he thought over Gram's words, which made even more sense as he reflected. He didn't really understand clinical depression, but knew Gram had bouts of it herself during his childhood. In her case, it was mostly caused by being a deeply religious person stuck in a bad marriage. Her health had miraculously improved once her husband passed away.

Putting the topic of depression aside, a decision would be made when Dave arrived on-site. At a minimum, he'd do a drive-by of their home to see how they were living. He'd have to get some more gift chocolate first, however.

The hotel in Los Banos was surprisingly good. There was even a Starbucks located on the way back to the freeway; an easy stop for breakfast on the way out. Dave sat down with his laptop and looked over satellite images of the area surrounding Becky and Steve's house. It was a modest single-family home, looking to have three bedrooms, one or two baths, with a single-car garage. In short, it appeared similar to any number of small ranch-style homes in California. Dave found a shopping mall close by their home and mapped a course for the next day's drive. He would take the time to swing by his fictional murder sites and get photos before deciding what to do about Becky.

Just to be fully transparent, Dave made sure to update his social media status, saying he was in route to the Sacramento area and would be there the next morning. Checking Becky and Steve's status, he saw they had been up to their usual banter within the last few hours. Perfect!

The next morning went according to plan. Dave had always taken good-natured ridicule from family members concerning the extent of his planning, but his life was smooth-running compared to the rest of them. It was a trade Dave would make anytime, given the amount of unnecessary drama which constituted the lives of those making the observations.

The murder sites he had selected proved to be perfect for the book promotion web pages, and Dave snapped many photos to be reviewed later. From there, it was a short hop to a shopping mall and obtaining a small gift box of boutique chocolates. It was a beautifully clear May day in Sacramento.

Today is so splendid it would be difficult to stay depressed, Dave thought. *No better time to foist myself on relatives.*

Feeling somewhat apprehensive, in spite of his preparations, Dave rehearsed what he planned to say when Becky opened the door. As he pulled into the neighborhood, there were children playing games in the street. He shook his head. When Dave was a child there weren't any nearby parks, so the street was the only decent flat open surface available. These kids had a fully equipped city park right around the corner, but here they were playing on old asphalt in front of their homes.

Parking on the street, he saw an old pickup truck in Becky's driveway. Looking closer, it had three flat tires and there was blown yard debris distributed around them. The truck hadn't moved in quite some time. It was parked squarely in front of the single-car garage, so if there was another car it hadn't been out of the garage in a long while either.

Dave stepped up to the door, and knocked firmly several times. The doorbell was missing a button and a disconnected wire jutted out in its place. There was no sound from inside the house. Dave expected there would be some barking by their dog, Buster, which he had seen online many times. Buster was supposed to be a fierce protector of the front door, but right now there was complete silence.

Dave knocked again. He heard nothing but the sounds of the children down the street. On impulse, Dave set down the chocolates and, using his mobile phone, accessed social media. Oddly enough, Becky had posted another one of her old family pictures not five minutes ago! Quickly, Dave posted a reply to her note, "Becky, where are you right now?"

Several minutes later, her reply came through, "At home, where else would I be?"

"I'm at your front door in Sacramento; been knocking for the last ten minutes. I come bearing chocolates!" Dave waited for a few minutes and the post was not answered. In fact, Becky signed off.

This is bullshit! I wonder what the hell is going on? Dave picked up the chocolates and walked around the house to see if there were any other signs of life: there were not. Something clearly was out of order here. Perhaps Becky and Steve had moved somewhere requiring less upkeep but, if so, no one had been told.

Dave was slowly working himself around to finding a way into the house. He walked up to the back door, which had a dog door inset and also looked as though it hadn't been used for a while. The dog door was secured, but Dave recognized the design and knew how to open it from the outside. With a few quick movements, the board blocking the dog door tumbled backwards into the house. Dave peered through the dark opening, unsure of what would greet his eyes.

The home was dark, but Dave could faintly make out a dusty kitchen area. A small kitchen table looked as though it had a layer of dirt, the dust was so thick. Making a decision, Dave reached in with his arm and unlocked the back door.

He entered the house, which was totally silent except for his footsteps. He jumped as the refrigerator compressor noisily kicked on and started running. Dave on impulse opened the refrigerator door, where he found empty space and nothing which appeared to be recent or edible. He opened the cupboards; they too were empty but for scattered rodent pellets and dust.

"Becky? Steve?" He called to no avail. It was strange, the electricity was on as well as the gas for the cook-top, yet the home seemed otherwise abandoned. There was water in the faucet, but it ran brown as though it hadn't been used in a while. Walking through the entire home, he found old, dusty furniture and empty space. The bedrooms sported beds without linens, one closet had women's clothes, and another held men's. There was a rusty dog crate in one corner of what was presumably Becky's room, but it was dust-covered as well, holding a sad water dish which had completed dried out. No Becky, no Steve, and no Buster. Checking out the main bathroom, the toilet had a ring indicating it hadn't been flushed in some time. The bathtub had a strange stain ring about six inches from the bottom, but also appeared otherwise unused.

Dave began to panic, wondering what he had gotten himself into. He turned hurriedly and decided he needed to leave the house behind. The house didn't show obvious signs of mayhem, but it was clear something wasn't right. He didn't plan on being one of those people who stand around something like this waiting for a sign from above. Better to get the hell away and talk to the authorities. Let the police sort it out!

Making sure he didn't touch anything else, Dave took a towel, which had seen better times, and used it to wipe the dog-door handles as well as the door knob. Kneeling down from outside, he replaced the dog door panel, then stood back to inspect the results. He was breathing heavily, as if his body knew something his mind did not, sweating bullets even though the morning itself wasn't warm.

A twig snapped suddenly behind him, and a baseball bat, hitting his head, punctuated his last conscious thought.

***

Sometime later, Dave awoke lying on his back in a strange position. His arms were secured to his torso by plastic zip ties, his legs were bound together in a similar fashion as well. Craning his neck around, he had been deposited into the dirty, ringed bathtub inside Becky's house. His mouth was gagged by a towel, his stomach heaved when he considered it might be the same dirty towel he had used earlier. Trying to get some leverage, Dave flexed his body trying to get out of the tub, making some small noises which sounded very loud in the silent house. He stopped struggling when he heard approaching footsteps.

"Ah, Dave, you're awake. I was beginning to think I hit you too hard," a male voice said, filled with the promise of violence.

Dave didn't recognize the voice and couldn't see its owner. There was an increasing scent of spent cigarettes as the stranger came closer. Dave tried turning his head around but it was no use.

"Rude of me to stand behind you. Here, I'll come around." A middle-aged man with graying, black hair came fully into Dave's field of vision and, closing the lid, sat down upon the toilet. His nondescript body argued for having been fit once, before aging turned the conditioning into something softer but still strong. There was nothing soft, however, about the dark brown eyes regarding Dave dispassionately.

"Dave, you just couldn't take 'no' for an answer, could you?"

Dave tried to reply, but the gag effectively made it unintelligible.

"I'm going to remove your gag, so we can have a small conversation. Obviously, if you shout or create any other disturbance I'll make you regret it. Nod your head if you understand me. Good!" The man stood and removed the gag from Dave's mouth then sat back down on the closed toilet.

Dave worked his stiff mouth for a few seconds, trying to get his saliva running once more. Finally, he managed a weak croak, "Who're you and what happened to my cousins?"

"Don't you recognize your dear cousin Becky? I know it's been a long time, but I would know you anywhere, Dave." The stranger affected a voice in a higher register.

"You're not Becky! Wait, are you Steve?"

"No, I'm not Steve," shaking his head in negation. "Actually, I'm the helpful next-door neighbor, Reggie, in one sense. In another much more lucrative way I am both of them."

"What did you do? Kill them and assume their identities?"

"It isn't as simple as that. Steve died of natural causes several years ago. I'd been helping Becky care for him doing the things requiring a bit more muscle around the house. Becky and I were in a relationship of sorts, mostly physical. You had one lusty cousin, I can testify to it personally! One night, we had a particularly loud session in her bedroom, and the next morning Steve was dead in his own bed. From what I could tell, he must have had a seizure while we were otherwise engaged. Becky was completely distraught, as she couldn't afford to continue living in the home without Steve's military pension. After giving it some thought, I suggested we dispose of Steve secretly and maintain the fiction of him being alive. We didn't kill him, after all. Eventually she came around and I disposed of the body."

"Wouldn't someone, one of his friends, have noticed?" Dave asked.

"No. As it turns out, he communicated with all of his friends by email and social media. These days, when telephone calls are finally mostly toll-free, people don't call. Becky helped craft Steve's responses to emails, and you've seen the results online. He's even one of your social media friends and you don't remember ever meeting him."

"What about the pension authorities? Wouldn't they notice?"

"No, they work off of death certificates and informants. There aren't enough of them to keep track of all of the recipients. We kept his bank accounts online, paid bills in his name, filed tax returns accurately and on-time; you get the idea. Becky kept up the charade until I got a feel for it and began to do most of the work myself."

"What happened to Becky?"

Reggie shrugged. "I didn't kill Steve, but I did help Becky on a little bit. About a year ago, she got sick herself, so much so she lost all interest in our other activities. That's when it occurred to me: Becky was receiving a social security check in addition to Steve's pension, why wouldn't I be able to collect both checks myself? Up until then, Becky had been banking the proceeds herself and primarily showing her gratitude in the bedroom. I learned a few things from disposing of Steve, and laced her herbal tea with a little something extra. It worked splendidly! I disposed of the body, maintained the normal cash flow through their accounts and acquired a nice little income stream for myself. Both of them were textbook shut-ins. Everyone who wants to see them is usually warned off with stories of diverticulitis and clinical depression. That is, until you showed up today," Reggie said.

Dave saw where this was headed and rushed to say, "People know I'm here! They'll ask questions if I disappear and investigate. You need to let me go, take what you've acquired, and depart for parts unknown ahead of the police."

"It's more complex, Dave. Since Becky and Steve met their respective ends, I've found a large number of similar elderly people who had few personal attachments. It's amazing how fast you can identify them, working as a volunteer helping shut-ins. I gain their trust and loyalty, then implement the same scenario. It's a full-time job: working all of the emails, bank accounts, and social media, to maintain the fiction of their continued existence. In the meantime, the deposits continue to come in. So, as you might understand, I'm not ready to walk away from it just yet."

"I won't tell anyone, I'll even help keep it going. Just let me go," Dave pleaded.

"I wish I could trust you with it, Dave," Reggie held up something in his hand. "Tell me, what is the swipe code to open your phone?"

Dave sat in shock, his mind scrambling for something, anything, which would result in him surviving the day. He decided to cooperate if only to play for time and told him.

"Thank you, very helpful. Let's see, mmm, you're currently logged into social media and email. Great, let's change your passwords to something I'll remember…very good. Tell me, Dave, do you bank online from your phone?"

Dave, recognizing his life was already lost, began to scream for help. Rolling his eyes, Reggie set the phone down and deliberately drew what appeared to be a surgical scalpel across Dave's neck in one clean movement. Dave's screams cut off as the blood began pumping out and ran down his body towards the drain.

Reggie bent over and placed a stopper in the tub drain. "I learned a lot from Steve, then Becky. It is best to let the body soak into a lye bath for several weeks. It keeps the smell down too, except for lye. I'll wait until you're gone before pouring the lye solution in, but you should make your peace now, Dave."

Dave struggled against his bonds, as life pumped out onto his chest before him. His breath gurgled through the cut as he tried to speak once more, perhaps in denial, or perhaps a curse. Before long the dizziness swept over him and he went away for good.

Humming a small tune to himself, something once sang by a group of merry dwarves in a Disney film, Becky/Steve/Dave/Reggie/Legion poured lye solution into the tub once more, careful to not splash any upon himself.

MOTHER OF DEMONS

Lucas eased his bulk back into the command chair of his Freightliner Coronado truck. He had pulled off onto a dirt road fifty miles outside of Barstow, California to dispose of a passenger in Southern California's trackless desert. The boy had fully served his purpose during the long ride from Columbus, Ohio. A runaway hitchhiker, fourteen or fifteen years old, Ryan was on his way to Las Vegas when Lucas offered a ride. Ryan took some beatings before he learned what Lucas wanted and became willing to give it up.

Early in the process, Lucas cuffed and shackled his passenger. At first, he needed gagging as well, until the hope was beaten out of him. Lucas fed him one meal per day and very little water. By the time they hit Vegas, the boy was barely alive, not responding when Lucas asked whether he wanted out there. Lucas had laughed, it was a game he understood well and generally he could keep unwilling passengers alive to the California State line. The trick was to use them up before hitting Barstow and leave their nude body under a bush in the desert. Generally, scavengers in the arid waste made short work of a body, and it saved the hot, sweaty effort of digging a hidden grave. Burying, while more hidden, tended to preserve a body longer - much longer. However, within a week of a body being desert-dumped, only a few well-chewed bones would remain.

Lucas loved his job driving cross-country freight, seldom did he ever break a sweat or deal with bosses telling him what to do. He did have the burden of a large, weekly payment for his truck, but as long as he kept moving, he could stay ahead of it. Dealing with dispatchers could be considered working for a boss, but it only happened two or three times a week, not nearly enough for Lucas to feel they were always on his case. Until this job, Lucas had never gone more than three months on any of them.

No; truck-driving paid the bills and left him free to pursue other interests.

When Lucas was in high school, it became clear no woman wanted anything to do with a six foot-two inch, 350 pound, goggle-eyed, moon-faced, receding hairlined man without being generously paid for it. Even churchwomen, who were obliged to be nice to fellow parishioners, didn't think of him in any interesting way. Getting some loving in church wasn't going to happen, even though he stayed involved there to keep his mother happy.

Lucas wasn't stupid, though, and when he applied his mind to the problem he came up with the perfect solution: male runaways. No one cares much about male runaways. If one vanishes, why, there were always more to choose from. Even when a body turned out to have been a male runaway, there wasn't much official interest beyond the perfunctory. Runaway girls are another matter; when alive their welfare isn't considered important enough to intervene, but if one is horribly killed, the National Guard is called up. Lucas noticed the discrepancy and used it to his advantage. After all, boys could deliver almost everything a girl could. *Two out of three ain't bad*, Lucas said to himself.

Having dropped off his most recent passenger, Lucas felt relaxed and ready to drive the final two hours to the destination truck terminal in Riverside, California. Once his trailer was unloaded, he'd be able to spend a couple of days at his mother's house before picking up a new load headed for the east coast.

Mom always welcomed her eldest son home with a big production. It was the one place Lucas was guaranteed respect for something other than his size and strength. Lucas was the most successful of all his siblings when it came to income. In fact, he was also more successful than either of his parents, even though the ever-present risk of his truck loan meant he had to keep moving in order to remain so. That modest financial success gave him a certain amount of swagger, and the discarded runaways contributed as well, to where he was almost insufferable to be around were it not for the bonds of family.

Lucas hummed as he drove Highway 15 towards Barstow, feet tapping out the miles. Behind, in the sleeper cab, a pair of red eyes watched his back. When headlights illuminated the cab, the eyes vanished but appeared once more in the complete darkness of evil deeds.

***

Lucas came in the front door of a small, frame house in the old Ontario neighborhood. The cheap frame and stucco homes had been built by returning GIs after WWII, four bedrooms and one bathroom on a postage stamp lot, one right after the other. Before being forcibly evicted, his Dad had added an additional small bathroom so that seven people could barely manage to live there. Three girls, two boys, Mom and Dad. Now, it was down to just Mom and her final underage son, Bennie.

"Luke, you're here!" a girl exclaimed as she opened the screen door and barreled into his arms. Relative to Lucas, she was small at 180 pounds in a 5'3" frame.

"Mantissa, what are you doing here?" Lucas asked his oldest sister. Their mother had decided the mathematics term she had heard in passing at school was a wonderful name for what was almost certainly a smart girl. Unfortunately, her hopes for intelligence had evolved in favor of remarkable self-esteem.

"Mom's having another of her episodes, so I came over to keep an eye on Bennie," Mantissa, or Tissa, clearly showed her relationship to Lucas but without the broad shoulders. Similarly moon-faced, with clear blue-eyes and a vacant expression.

"Shit, how long has she been in there this time?"

"About two days, Bennie called me yesterday."

A small monstrosity came down the hall from the general direction of Mom's room, exuding an evil aura as it came.

"What the fuck is that, another goddam demon? Didn't we get this place exorcised just last month?" Lucas asked as he reached for the silver cross worn around his neck.

"I haven't seen this one before, it's new. They just keep coming back like cockroaches," Mantissa had her own cross in hand as the demon quickly shied away passing through the living room and out the front door into a more congenial world.

"We'll have to get Reverend Bob out here again, but should probably wait until Mom is up and about," Lucas said matter-of-factly. "You making dinner?"

"I am."

"Great, I'll go look in on her and see how she's doing," Lucas said as he walked up the hall. As he got closer to the master bedroom he could hear his mother whimpering in pain. Mom suffered from self-diagnosed fibromyalgia and, while medicated most of the time, seemed to still have periods where nothing helped. She would confine herself to bed for several days until feeling well enough to re-emerge. Tapping softly at the door, he opened it quietly and stepped inside the room.

It was dark, as it usually was whenever the headaches took her and any light hurt her eyes. A warm, wet ambiance prevailed, with the sickly sweet smell of flop sweat. Her head, propped up on several pillows, listed as she twitched and whimpered with pain. Margritte, or Margie, was once a comely young woman, more than enough to attract Lucas' father. He was a few years older, and knew the disparity of intelligence could be a future problem but overlooked it in favor of her beautiful face and youthful charms.

Margie had a way of wearing an appearance of empathy as a substitute for higher thought. She would come up to a person, ask after their current personal life oozing smarmy sincerity, dark brown eyes sucking the victim in and relishing every secret thereby acquired. People who recoiled at her approach were labeled with whatever negative psychology term she had read about that week. In short, she was custom-made to be a church lady and gossip maven, ministering to the faithful. During her marriage, she had started college several times, thinking she could easily do the coursework for psychology given her self-assessed innate talents. Alas, even the least reputable schools required a minimum of scholarship, so her fondest wish of gaining a therapist certification was not to be. She made do with the rush of being a social worker and volunteer to the less fortunate instead.

Margie spent more and more of her time on the woes of others until her marriage suffered. After a full day of empathy, she was too tired to join her husband in connubial bliss. After several years of being thus denied, he found a mistress who specialized in such things. When Margie learned of the affair, she gained the wronged woman martyrdom medal and wore it proudly, throwing her husband to the curb. Now she had her own sad stories to tell, and pity to reap.

None of the pride was present now, as she lay sweating with sheets pulled into a bunch between columnar thighs underneath sweating pendulous breasts. Her breasts were completely exposed but for nipples, hidden solely because the nipples were stuck to her stomach. The massive belly jiggled like Jello with no muscle tone, or a woman who had just given birth. Margie's face, no longer beautiful, forehead broad like those of her children, fat cheeks running with sweat, teeth yellowed from too much herbal tea, and eyes once doe-like now resemble those of a cow on its way to slaughter.

The eyes fluttered, "Lucas? You're here?"

"I am, what the hell is going on with you, Mom?"

"The pain, the pain is too much. Drugs aren't helping. I fired my doctor, he didn't believe I was in pain. Curse the man, he went and canceled all of my prescriptions. The new doctor only gave me half doses to be cautious at first. So I'm having to take the pain without help. In a couple of days, I hope I'll be able to sweat things out and be back to my old self. I'm glad you're here though. How long can you stay this time?"

"Not long. I have the weekend, but then need to head back east with another load. Your son has a truck loan with weekly payments, can't stop for very long. That's my dark reality, Mom." Lucas said, thinking this visit was going to be a bust if no one was going to be taking care of him.

"Your cousin Bethany is back from college this weekend, you kids ought to see if you can't go out to dinner to catch up. Maybe get some Mexican food in San Dimas, that place we like. You could even bring me something back."

"Mantissa was talking about making dinner, but I could really go for some Mexican food. A couple of margaritas would go down well, too. I'll see if Tissa is up for it. Mom, we just saw another demon pass through the living room, have you seen anything?"

"No, I haven't, but you know I'm out of my mind when the pain hits. I'm lucky to be able to talk to you, in between the surges of pain. Look at me, still sweating like it's summer in Houston," she ineffectually pulled at soggy sheets to better conceal her flaccid bulk.

"Just rest and I'll get some ice water," Lucas said and stepped into the hallway.

He walked into the kitchen where Tissa was starting to check out the contents of their mother's mostly empty refrigerator. "She hasn't done much shopping in recent days, I'll have to go get her and Bennie some food it looks like."

"Hold off on that, Mom just said Cousin Bethany was in town this weekend, and maybe we should all hit the Mexican place tonight. We'll take Benny of course and get Mom some takeout. I haven't seen Bethany in a few years." Bethany and Tissa were of an age, but that's where the comparisons stopped. Bethany had been a high school cheerleader on the honor roll and while Tissa hit her peak when it came to attractiveness during those years, Bethany was in a different league. Lucas was beginning to see some potential for the weekend after all, Bethany had been sexy as hell when she was in high school and should be even better now.

"She is, I was planning go to church with her on Sunday, but this plan is much more fun," Tissa said excitedly.

"Call her up! Tell her I'm buying, that should make it easier." Lucas knew few people in their family could resist a free meal. Tissa took her phone and started exchanging texts.

"She can meet us there at 6, is that alright?" Tissa asked.

"Sure, gives us time to roust Bennie and get some groceries. I'll take Mom some ice water and let her know we'll be leaving. Meet back here in fifteen." Lucas walked back down the hall, softly opening his mom's door. She was back in the throes of dealing with her pain. He set the glass down on her night stand and left the room as silently as he had entered.

Outside Bennie's room he tapped once then opened the door, knowing Bennie would barely notice his presence. Bennie sat at a work table next to his bed, assembling something with Legos. As usual, the borderline-autistic Bennie was completely dialed into the task and didn't hear Lucas come into the room. Lucas moved into Bennie's line of vision and waited.

"Lucas, you're here," Bennie said with his normal flat affect. Bennie was the spitting image of Lucas when starting high school. The last two years had seen a spurt of growth in height, but the body had yet to fill into what would also be a large frame. Margie had decided years earlier that Bennie was destined to be an engineer, because he liked to build Lego projects. She didn't reckon on the real requirements for engineers, namely a vast capacity for science and math, which Bennie didn't seem to possess at all. Margie had her son in every "autism" program there was in her price range, in spite of being told Bennie wasn't full-on autistic.

"Come-on, Bud. We're going to get some Mexican food with Cousin Bethany, so get cleaned up and be ready before 6. Tissa and I are going to hit the supermarket beforehand; the refrigerator is close to empty," Lucas said.

Bennie's hands never stopped moving as he assembled Legos, "Mom is sick again and demons have come back. Bethany has nice tits."

"I know about the demons, and since you notice tits now, I'll make sure to seat you on the other side of the table so you can see better," Lucas said to the unresponsive back of Bennie's head. Shaking his head, Lucas went back out to the kitchen to find his sister. Tissa drove to the local supermarket and they filled a shopping cart with all of the essentials.

"Lucas, we might want to get Reverend Bob back before mom gets better, it might be a while and all those demons are a problem. They shouldn't be around Bennie like that," Tissa said.

"I don't know what you're worried about, that boy is about as brainless as any I know. What demon in their right mind would want to possess him?"

"He wears his crucifix, so he should be safe from that. I'm more worried about them whispering evil things into his ear. You should hear some of the filth they've said to me," Tissa said as her face colored in embarrassment.

"Oh? Do tell," Lucas scoffed.

"Horrible things, things I can't tell anyone, even a preacher. Sex-stuff."

"What kind of sex stuff?"

"Things they want me to do so they can watch, they even want to have sex," Tissa said with a shudder.

"You'd probably feel differently if one or more of them were handsome. I know I would have no trouble going there if it were an attractive female demon. These stunted little ones we seem to get in our home aren't that. But now that I think about it, their organs always seem larger than they should be given their small size..."

"Hush," Tissa said looking around the supermarket in case someone was listening.

Lucas laughed and let the conversation drop. He turned his mind on what he would have to do if Bethany turned out to be anything as sexy as she was the last time. When they were all kids playing games, she had always loved her older cousin Lucas and sat in his lap. Maybe he would be getting something wet this weekend after all. Perhaps he should pick up some love-oil from the truck just-in-case. "Say, on the way back, can we swing by my truck, I need to pick up a few things I forgot."

"Sure, where did you park it?"

Lucas directed Tissa as she drove to the long-term truck parking lot off the interstate. She stopped next to it and waited while Lucas jumped up into the cab to get what he needed. A few seconds later, he came down carrying a small bag like those used for liquor bottles.

"Lucas, what is that demon doing in your truck?" Tissa asked.

"What demon?"

"That one, there! In the shadows behind your driver's seat."

"You're losing it, Tiss! I don't see anything."

"It's right there, where it could whisper to you while you drive. You don't see it?"

"No, and you do?"

"Yes. It looks like an evil one."

"They're all evil, Tissa."

"There's evil and then there's *evil*. This is a bad one, mark my words. Get Reverend Bob to exorcize your truck before you leave, Lucas, please!"

"Sure thing, sis!"

"What did you forget?"

"Ah, shaving stuff, toothbrush. I just forgot to put it in my overnight bag."

Tissa drove back to their old home and restocked the refrigerator with food. They could easily make the restaurant on-time if they left right away. Lucas swung by Bennie's room and came back with him in tow. Bennie was carrying a portable Lego kit and clearly planned to keep himself occupied.

A few miles later, they pulled into the El Azteca restaurant parking lot. Bethany and her brother Frank waved from the front door as Tissa found a parking spot.

Lucas was gratified to see Bethany had grown up but not out. She was wearing patterned shorts displaying most of her toned legs and an artfully unbuttoned blouse hugged her form but didn't give anything away. If Lucas hadn't known better, he would think she had gotten a boob job, but she'd had the beginnings of it even when she was a teenager.

Lucas, Tissa, and Bennie lumbered up to the restaurant door.

"Lucas, I haven't seen you in a while," Bethany held open her arms for a chaste hug and air-kissed his cheek.

Lucas was on his best behavior, as he reciprocated. "You too, Bethany! How're you doing, Frank?" Lucas made a big deal of shaking Frank's hand before opening the restaurant door for the group to enter. 6 pm was early enough that a booth was open immediately and so the whole crew sat right down. True to his word, Lucas arranged things so that Bethany and he sat on one side of the booth while Bennie sat next to Tissa, opposite Bethany. Lucas took up two-thirds of the space on their side and found he, too, had a great view down Bethany's blouse.

The waiter dropped off menus and tortilla chip baskets, which the cousins dug into immediately. Everyone ordered a margarita, except for Bennie, and soon the conversations took off. Evidently, Bethany was pre-med at one of the better colleges in the area. She still found something worthwhile to talk about with Tissa, in spite of their now very different lives. Frank wanted to know all about long-haul trucking. Lucas was happy to regale his cousin with stories of the road.

After a couple of margaritas, Lucas decided it was time to do some bragging to establish himself as more than Bethany's equal. "You know, Bethany, I was headed for college to do something like you, but realized pretty quickly it would take a really long time to do better than starting work instead. We didn't have a lot of money at the time, too. No, I looked at how much the loans would be, it took ten years to get the right certifications, then would take another ten years to pay off the loans. So I ended up starting my own business instead. I do miss the idea of spending the time in college, everyone says it is a great experience, it just seemed like it would better to start living now."

"Yeah, the loans are brutal. You know my folks don't have a lot of money either, but they kick in a little bit. I get a combination of scholarship grants and loans. It isn't too bad right now, but med-school will be expensive. But I've always wanted to do it, and I can, so I am," Bethany said.

Frank piped up, "Bethany will owe the family free medical advice when she's a doctor."

"Bethany, you know about Mom's fibromyalgia, right? What do you think about that?" Tissa asked.

"I don't know much about it, although it has come up a couple times in my classes. It's one of those things we don't know much about, kind of like Legionnaires Disease; no one really knows what causes it or how to treat it other than pain meds. Brain specialists don't consider it in their scope either, some even think it's psychological in nature. But there is no denying physiological changes occur in the brain and there is pain."

"Wow, I'd love to see the look on Mom's face if we told her it's all in her head," Lucas said and snorted.

"I didn't say that! It might start there, but once the patient has it there isn't much that works. Stress or physical injury is one of the theories. I'm finding when doctors don't know why, they seem to say it's stress," Bethany said and smiled.

"Speaking of stress relief, do you still have that old boyfriend? You were planning to go to college together, right?" Lucas pried.

"Oh, Timmy? He's long gone, he actually went to a school specializing in engineering. Bennie, are you still thinking about doing that?" Bethany tried to pull the shy boy into the conversation. Bennie was assembling and disassembling various Lego configurations, periodically glancing at Bethany before dropping his eyes.

Lucas was having a fabulous time glancing down Bethany's blouse. The cleavage provided more than enough room for him to have a great view. He, too, worked on keeping the pervy impulse to himself, by only looking for short periods. Their meal arrived quickly, as always, and the cousins dove into the delicious meal.

Afterwards, Lucas decided he wanted some pictures of Bethany for later perusal and suggested the waiter take pictures. Lucas put his arm around her and pulled her close for the photos. Bethany seemed a bit surprised, but quickly shook it off as they all smiled for the camera. Immediately after, she moved back into her own space, seeming to shrink. Lucas left his arm on the back of Bethany's seat and waxed jovial with yet another margarita. When the bill came, Lucas took the check in a flashy way, paying cash off of a roll of hundred dollar bills he kept for situations like this. For some reason, dropping a credit card didn't impress the babes as much as large denomination cash. *More where this came from, honey!* Unfortunately Bethany wasn't fixated on the cash as she chatted animatedly with Tissa. Frank liked the look of it, but he was probably just jealous.

The group finished up and stood carefully. Lucas had the most drinks, but he was also a lot heavier than everyone else. They exited the restaurant and stood around a little more.

"Bethany, you ought to come see my truck before we both leave town. Have you ever been inside a big rig?" Lucas asked.

"I don't know, Lucas, things are pretty busy this weekend. I have some friends from college coming in tomorrow morning and we'll all go back together on Sunday. Our place will be pretty crowded, but it should be fun. I'd like a raincheck on that one, if you don't mind," Bethany said. She hadn't missed Lucas' pervy moves during the entire meal and had decided to not be alone with him at all.

"Well, whatever. I thought you might like it is all." Lucas was trying and failing to guilt her into changing her mind.

"I'd like to see it sometime," Frank said eagerly.

"Sounds like you're going to be pretty busy over there, Frank. But if you get bored, send me a text and I'll take you to see it." Lucas figured racking up a little bit of admiration in Frank wouldn't be a bad thing either. He'd have to be picked up and then Lucas could check out Bethany's college friends, too.

"I'd like to see it again, if Frank goes," Bennie spoke up furtively while still sneaking glances of Bethany.

Lucas snorted and walked back to Tissa's car. They waved as Bethany and Frank drove off, then headed home themselves.

"Do you think Mom will be any better?" Bennie asked.

"We'll have to see. I have some chips and enchiladas for her, that usually cheers her up," Tissa said.

They pulled onto the cracked concrete driveway which had weeds coming through from below. No lights were on in the house, which was odd, since Lucas distinctly remembered leaving several on. Tissa inserted her key into the lock and turned the knob to open the door. It opened with a sticky, wet, pop sound which Lucas immediately associated with a human body past its expiration date. It had only happened once that he kept a body two extra days after death thinking it would be more secure to dump it further away. The cleanup had been horrendous. The truck cab got hot when Lucas stepped out for anything, and the body had almost melted. Nope,

Lucas learned the lesson in one sitting, get rid of the body soon after death. The door making a similar sound was not a good sign.

Tissa veered off to turn on a table lamp, stepping in something wet as she did. "Ugh, gross, what is this goop?" Tissa said as the light came on.

"It looks like that slime from Ghostbusters. Bennie, stay out of that," Lucas ordered as Bennie stretched a finger toward the nasty, viscous fluid.

"Look, there's more in the hall. Seems like it was tracked in by little feet," Tissa said.

"I'm going to check on Mom. Tissa, you and Bennie start cleaning this up," Lucas ordered. He walked cautiously down the hall, attempting to keep the goo off of his sneaks. Margie's bedroom door was ajar and inside puddles of goo covered most of the floor. Lucas could dimly see a whimpering mound upon the bed. Reaching over to the light switch, he flipped it on.

Light flared and then strangely dimmed as Lucas made out his mother, completely nude now, on her back with her legs spread, in a grotesque parody of a birthing position. Inarticulate whimpering came in phases, almost in tune with the contractions Lucas could see rippling across her belly, down from under her pendulous breasts. Incredibly, it looked like something was happening to Margie's swollen vagina, as though she was giving birth. Lucas knew his mother hadn't had sex in more than a few years, and looking at her, who would want to?

"Mom, what's happening to you?" Lucas asked urgently. She didn't reply, only keening sounds came from her mouth, face showing no signs of awareness of anything more than her labor. Now Lucas' eyes had adjusted to the reduced light and he saw the fluid goo came from within her vagina, a veritable river of it soaked the end of the bed, dripping down onto the floor. Lucas knew this wasn't right, he'd witnessed a woman giving birth once at a truck stop, and while there was extra fluid there wasn't very much of it. This bed and floor looked as though gallons had come forth.

The cries increased in tempo, each grouping louder and higher pitched than the one before it.

Lucas went back to the door and hollered down the hall, "Tissa, get in here! Send Bennie to his room."

By the time Tissa had come clomping down the hall and came into the room, something had begun to emerge from Margie's vagina: long, pointed ears and a darkly nacreous head. It was a demon, a small demon, very much like the one they had seen earlier. The head and shoulders, once emerged, were then used to push itself completely out of its mother's womb, leaving the imprint of small, clawed hands upon her turgid flesh.

Lucas looked for something to kill the demon, and came up empty. Once more, he took up his silver crucifix and pressed it into the recovering demon spawn's skin which was becoming dark and leathery as Lucas watched. This demon hissed at Lucas, but was not put off much by the contact, certainly not as much as Lucas would have expected. Tissa pulled hers out as well, and did the same. This time the demon wailed in pain, scrambling up off of the bed and for the door.

Lucas and Tissa followed, hoping to be able to score more hits upon the intruder. It proved faster and blasted a small hole through the front door in its haste to escape. Without stopping to think, they turned back to Margie's room.

As Lucas feared, their mother was already beginning to birth another one, the next few hours were a complete fiasco. A demon would be birthed and the two humans would do their best to encourage its immediate departure. Margie wasn't coherent during this process, saying nothing a human might say, just keening when it came time to birth another demon. Lucas and Tissa were covered in the strange funky fluid. Bennie had retired to his room and as far as Lucas could determine was no longer paying attention to anything outside. *That kid is gonna have to pull his head out of his ass at some point. I'm not buying this autism bullshit!*

"Tissa, why the hell isn't my cross doing much damage to the demons? I have to club 'em to get their attention."

"That's strange. Have you committed any major sins while wearing it? I always take mine off when I go out on a date. Plus, Reverend Bob blessed mine recently too. How long ago was yours done?"

"Probably the last time Reverend Bob was over when I was here. Probably ought to get him over here, this is more than we can handle. I hope Mom comes out of this OK," Lucas said, thinking about how he had worn the crucifix during his sexual encounters with the unwilling hitchhikers. Hell, he had even been wearing it when he finally killed them off. He'd have to remember that next time.

"Do you think Mom has been the one behind all of the demons. You know, we never really bother her when she has her episodes. Lucas, Reverend Bob needs to see this for himself. I'll go call him."

"Do that, but hurry back, she looks like she is winding up for more."

Three demons were birthed in quick succession. Each time they were met by the full force and effect of Lucas swinging a baseball bat he snagged from his old room. The crucifix wasn't working, time to try something else. *Maybe Reverend Bob could bless the bat; that would send these bastards into next week.* Without the blessing, the weak demons were merely hurt temporarily and herded towards the front door which was now left open.

Reverend Bob arrived about an hour later, he'd been asleep when Tissa's frenzied call came. By now the buzz of the margaritas was long gone, and Lucas looked as though he had fought his way through a vat of snot. Tissa didn't look much better.

"OK, children; show me what we're dealing with and to Jesus be the glory!" Reverend Bob was carrying what looked like a small medical bag in one hand and his trusty King James Bible in the other. Lucas was too tired to argue about the children comment, beckoning the man of God down the hall towards the portal to hell which Margie had become.

"My God, Margritte, what has the devil done to you?" Reverend Bob looked for a clean spot to set his bag and finding none chose a side chair. Margie gave no indication she heard anything and started the panting which her children had learned meant birthing was imminent.

Reverend Bob began muttering prayers under his breath holding his Bible up above his head while his other hand was placed upon Margie's forehead. "In the name of Jesus Christ of Nazareth, I command you, demon, to depart."

Margie gave no indication there was any effect to the casting out, and her panting escalated into the high-pitched cries.

"Quick, Reverend Bob, bless this bat before she gives birth again. My crucifix doesn't work anymore," Lucas said.

"Sins, my boy, sins. Here, give me the bat." Reverend Bob closed his eyes in prayer while holding onto the bat, asking God to bless both the bat and the person who used it for God's glory. He handed it back to Lucas just as the new demon started to emerge. Lucas stood ready to hit it as it cleared his mother's body.

Once more, Reverend Bob used the tried and true formulation, "In the name of Jesus Christ of Nazareth, I command you, demon, to depart." The demon wailed a pitiful sound and ran for the door, but not before Lucas hit it a mighty clip with the bat knocking it temporarily senseless into the hallway. Tissa chose that moment to press her crucifix against the exposed demon skin. Jumping up, the demon screamed and ran for the open door as had all the others.

"Thank you, Reverend! That blessing knocked him right out of the room. I was having to hit them four or five times before. This is a lot better," Lucas said.

Margie had resumed her low-level panting amid the morass of her bed.

"Son, how long has she been like this?"

"Tissa said it was a couple of days, not like this exactly, but with her fibromyalgia episodes. She usually is in bed for several days when that happens. We've never seen her do this before," Lucas said.

"I wondered where all the demons were coming from, I've had to cleanse this house four to five times. I'm relieved to see it isn't the same demons coming back. My cleansing should send them back to the hell they come from, but if all it did was disperse them it could be a real problem. I've never seen a human woman give birth to a demon. I didn't even know it was possible."

"Reverend Bob, Lucas has a demon in his truck, too, but he couldn't see it. I saw it plain as day behind the driver's seat," Tissa piped up.

Reverend Bob turned to look at Lucas, "People don't see the demons they listen to, that's how a demon gains entry into your body. Lucas, have you had sinful urges or thoughts more often lately?"

Lucas didn't want to be on this topic for very long, "No more than usual. I don't know what Tissa is talking about, I didn't see any demon up there. The kind of urges I get are the natural ones when I see a pretty girl. I get to church every time I'm in town, but it's hard to do on the road."

"Common lust wouldn't explain a demon's continued presence. I'll go out there with you after we see your momma straight. Look, she's winding up for another round. Tissa, get a big pot of water and bring it back. Lucas, stand ready to smack down more minions of the evil one!" Reverend Bob rallied his troops.

The next few minutes were very similar to the last birth. Reverend Bob's exorcism weakened or slowed the newly emerged demon while Lucas applied the bat to finish the job. The demons were not going back to hell, however, just out the front door.

Tissa picked that moment to return with a stock pan full of water. Reverend Bob took the water and began the process of blessing it. Lucas wiped off the demon ichor which coated his bat. Tissa talked to Margie who still lay unresponsive to anything other than the internal needs of her ravaged body.

Reverend Bob finished up and moved the pot closer to the bed, "Stand back Tissa, I'm going to douse her in some of this blessed water, it might bring her up enough to talk to us." With that he began pouring the water on Margie from her head down towards her waist. She had no reaction to the water until it began to splash her lower belly. She screamed aloud and convulsed as something alive inside her reacted to the presence of the water. The violent reaction continued as it fought to exit the host body.

Reverend Bob poured the last of the water along each of her exposed columnar legs, taking care to bathe all of the exposed skin. He was surprised the water hadn't pained Margie herself. His first theory was that she had given herself over to evil, and the water should have been very painful in that case. It was obviously painful to whatever was alive inside her, but not to Margie herself.

"This place is a fucking mess – sorry, Reverend." Lucas was beginning to tire of the entire situation. It had been fun for a while to kick the crap out of some small demons, but now it was beginning to feel like a job. The prospect of getting into Bethany's easy-access shorts seemed less and less likely. He'd be damned if he had to hang around this loser's nest for an entire weekend. Normally, Lucas would have his feet up in the living room watching a game or something else on the TV while his mom made a big deal about him. This wasn't what he signed on for, and on the road at least he could make some money while bored out of his mind.

"We're all stretched to our limits, son. I'm sure God takes it into account. Did your mom make any reference to a new romantic interest in her life?"

"No way," Lucas said.

"No, Reverend. When I would ask about it, she always told me the pain from her fibromyalgia made anything like romance unthinkable. No one has been hanging around either. It's just been her and Bennie," Tissa weighed in.

"Where are the others?"

"I'm not sure, Bryan ran away a couple years ago, haven't heard from him at all. Jenni was living on the streets doing drugs the last time I heard. She was hard on meth at one point and we just lost touch. I doubt I would recognize her now, she looked rough when I saw her last year. Mom threw her out when she wouldn't do rehab after stealing our stuff." Tissa didn't seem particularly put out to be missing two of her siblings.

Must be something about this family, Reverend Bob thought to himself. *They have the outward appearance of a family but each is more about themselves. Tissa is well-meaning if somewhat dim, Lucas could be anything. There is more to the Lucas story and it involves something other than lusting after truck-stop hookers. He might be involved in organized crime somehow, a lot of truckers do things to supplement their income. I'll see what's hiding in his truck and maybe then we'll know.*

The creature within Margie subsided as she started the panting which accompanied each birth, once more the team ushered another demon out into the night. As Lucas came back into the room after encouraging the demon down the hallway, Margie stirred.

"Reverend, you're here?" Margie asked weakly as she gathered the wet sheets in a futile late attempt at modesty.

"Yes, Miss Margie, I'm here with Tissa and Lucas. How are you feeling?"

"Better than before, I had another attack didn't I?"

"You did. Tissa, get your mom something to drink, she needs it." Reverend Bob was determined to get to the bottom of what was happening, Margie was one of his most fervid supporters in church. He needed to understand how someone like her could be in such a situation.

"Now, Margie, do you remember anything from tonight at all?"

"No, Reverend Bob. I remember waves of pain, like the tide coming in. It would go away for a little bit then come back. What was happening, I must have sweated a storm with how wet everything is, and is that blood?"

"Yes, it is. Margie, I don't know any other way to say this but out front, the pains you felt were those of giving birth," Reverend Bob said.

"Giving birth, how could I be giving birth? I'm old and you know there has been no man in my life since my husband left. Besides where is the baby?" Margie was beginning to become upset.

"Tissa, get a bowl of warm water and some washcloths to help clean up your mother please," Reverend Bob ordered. Tissa scurried out of the room in search of the requested items, ashamed she had not thought of it herself.

After she left the room, Reverend Bob reached forward and touched Margie's hand. "Margie, Lucas and I are here with you. You're safe. I want you to brace yourself, though, because this will not be pleasant to hear. There was more than one baby, and unfortunately they are almost certainly still with us. You've been giving birth to those small demons which have infested your home. In a bit, Lucas here and I are going back to his truck because Tissa said she saw one there earlier tonight."

"What are you saying, my fibromyalgia pain blackouts are giving birth? Again, how can I be giving birth when there is no father?"

"When did the demons start showing up? I don't claim to understand it either, Margie, but you have to admit there is a kind of logic to it. But we all know Satan is the father of demons."

"Are you saying I'm having sex with Satan the deceiver? I haven't had intercourse at all since my husband left. You don't think I'm the mother of demons, do you?"

"Maybe you were asleep, Margie. Have you ever woken up feeling as though you had been violated? There is no way it happened without carnal knowledge, only God can father a son within a virgin. The alternative is that you simply cannot remember it."

"Reverend, some of those demons whose asses we kicked were female," Lucas pointed out.

"Son, not helpful. Margie, going back to my original question, when did the demons start showing up? It was several years ago, right? You called me in sometime around then. Was that the beginning?"

"No, there were other preachers who helped us before. Eventually they would give up, the demons kept coming. You're the first to stick it out, God bless you."

"Alright, when did the fibromyalgia start?"

"I can answer that," Lucas said, "it was about the time Dad got remarried. Mom was depressed and the next thing we knew she started having the attacks. It got worse when he started having more kids."

"Anyone would be depressed. I had you kids to raise, and no prospects for anything else."

"Mom, you got the house and monthly alimony payments. Now, it's an old house, but it's still a house you own outright in California. Bennie will be old enough to be on his own in a few years, heck, he could even drive a truck if it came to that."

"Margritte, I don't believe you're possessed by Satan. My holy water and blessings didn't affect you and they would have if you were the Devil's. I have many women in the church with fibromyalgia and there have been many demon sightings there. I wonder how many are suffering the same infusion of the demonseed, birthing the spawns of Satan?" Reverend Bob said.

"There is something I barely remember, Reverend. When I've been in the worst pain sometimes I would hear a voice in the dark, asking if I wanted relief from the pain.

Sometimes, I say yes, Reverend. Anything to end it. But there are none of the normal evidences of intercourse, and I thought it was God, because I had been praying." Margie broke down in tears.

"Bless you, Margie. I think we have something there which is how Satan came to you. He waited until you were weak with pain and praying for relief. The deceiver that he is, he pretended to be God the Almighty himself, and took the permission he needed. It wasn't your fault, dear girl, there is a reason he is called the deceiver. God must have wanted us all to learn this lesson, Bless His Name! Let us pray now for strength to resist the wiles of the Devil, for we are weak without our Lord and Savior Jesus Christ!"

Everyone but Margie dropped to their knees beside the still-swamped bed in prayer. Reverend Bob found the words from somewhere, preach-praying for more than thirty minutes. He rose shakily to stand on his feet. One hand he placed on Lucas, the other on Tissa. "Lord, bless these children who loving their mother, want to save her from the Devil's snares. Give them the strength to raise her up and hold her close to the glory of our Lord Jesus Christ, Amen!"

Lucas looked up with a wonder different from his usual cynical self. A new life seemingly beckoned to him, one where he could earn the approval of others by doing something he particularly enjoyed, kicking the asses of demons.

"Reverend Bob, how are we going to deal with all the demon attacks. So far it has been just my mom, if what you suspect is true we could have a real problem here. How can I help?" Lucas asked.

"We'll need you and a few other strong warriors of Christ to win this battle. I think your Mom will be fine for a while, especially if Tissa sits in with her now. Miss Margie, will you be able to rest now, do you think?"

"I think the attack is over for now, I should be alright for two to three weeks if the past is any indication. Go do what needs to be done and come back when you can," Margie said from her pillows.

"Come, lad. Let's go to your truck. Bring the bat, we might need it. I'll drive my car." Walking back towards the front door, Lucas cracked the door to Bennie's room to check in on him. The boy was dead asleep atop his bed, which was much better than either man had hoped given all of the noise of the last few hours.

"Bennie is a concern, too, Reverend. Sometimes I'm not sure whether he is autistic or merely dim. You don't think the demons have a hold on him, too? He was alone with mom for a couple of days before Tissa came over," Lucas said.

"We'll check into that later, right now we need to see what is up with your truck. Ah, here we are, where are you parked?"

Lucas pointed out where his rig was sitting feeling some concern. Reverend Bob might be able to discern the horrors which had been perpetrated within it. God knows he had never seen a demon there in the past.

Lucas, a spectral voice whispered. *Lucas, take the bat and kill the Reverend. He wants to trap you into confessing your sins, then everything will end.*

The voice sounded familiar in a way Lucas could not explain. Reverend Bob looked over the rig seemingly unable to hear the voice.

Am I going crazy? Lucas asked himself.

No, idiot! But if the preacher has his way, there won't be any more road-pussy for you. Then you'll go to jail or back to being a fat Sunday School freak show again. How much pussy do you think will be there then, hmm? Do you think Bethany will open her legs for you or turn her lips in disgust? A filthy man-child with filthy habits.

We don't confess our sins to anyone but God, demon! We're not fucking Catholics!

"Reverend, the demon is talking to me, asking me to do horrible things; help me!" Lucas blurted out.

Reverend Bob splashed holy water onto Lucas' forehead, "Let the water blessed be your shield against the wiles of the ungodly demon scum and clear the scales from your eyes."

"There it is, right behind my seat. I can see it now. Back me up, I'm going to roust him out of there." Lucas heaved his bulk up into the cab, swinging his holy bat against the small, insidious creature, most swings hitting the side of the cab in a horrendous din. Finally, he connected solidly and the imp wailed in pain as it scrabbled for the door and freedom. It ran right into a waiting preacher man bearing the holy water of almighty Jesus in a handy squirt bottle. Skin smoking, the demon ran out of the parking lot and soon was out of sight.

"Did you get him, Reverend?"

"I did. I don't think that demon will be back to plague you, son. Tell me, how did the demon tempt you?"

Lucas climbed down off of the truck before answering, "It's embarrassing, it promised the love of women and knew it was hard for me to get anywhere there, given my size."

"Ah, youth. Love and affection is very important, especially to those Christ holds dear. Is there no one special in your life?"

"No, Reverend. I travel too much and it's hard to meet people."

"I guess it depends on how you travel, Lucas. Tell me, how would you feel if you became my own right hand in the struggle against Satan's minions? You would have to give up your trucking job, but we would still be traveling from church to church."

"How would I pay my bills? I need the trucking income to get by."

"Oh ye of little faith! Why do you think we'd be going from church to church? To spread God's word, of course, and collect church cash contributions to do our great work. We'd come in and give a presentation then ask for support. I'll split the take 70/30 with you. Even your 30% will wind up being a lot of money. Plus, the young women of such churches are so impressed with young men of God, they've been known to commit fornication without thought for the consequences. They also don't worry much about looks, as long as we're dressed well."

"Isn't fornication a sin, Reverend?"

"It is, but remember two things. First, God created sex to be enjoyable for a reason and, second, God will forgive your sins if you confess them in humble prayer, no matter what the sin. All men are tempted and occasionally give in to temptation. Women do the same. When I was a traveling evangelist in the 80s, married women were the most likely to knock on my hotel room door after the service. Look at me, I've never been extremely attractive, but I can make a woman feel close to God. Lucas, believe me, there is a market waiting for a big strapping man of God like yourself."

"What do I have to do?"

"First, let's lock up your truck," Reverend Bob said with a smile. "Give me the bat, we can do this the way it was done during the crusades. Now, kneel and take a moment to converse with God. Confess all of your sins, all of them, and ask forgiveness."

Lucas knelt down, and asked God's forgiveness for every sin he could think of committing during his interstate serial killing spree. He even threw in lusting and scheming over Bethany. After all, a clean slate is a clean slate. A feeling of profound lightness permeated his being. Who knew his sins were weighing him down as much as they were? Opening his eyes, he looked up at Reverend Bob in wonder.

"Alright, Lord Jesus, we have before us Lucas who is clean as driven snow under your grace. He wants to accept your calling as a warrior of God, to smite and cleanse the demon scourge from this land. Lucas, do you renounce the works of Satan and promise to devote your life to the battle against his evil works?"

"I do, Reverend."

"Then by the grace of the Lord Jesus Christ, I welcome you as the first called to our brotherhood. I anoint you as God's chosen with holy waters," Reverend Bob squirted holy water on Lucas' forehead. "Take this Blessed Bat as your first weapon to destroy the unholy, in the name of the Father, the Son, and the Holy Ghost. Amen! Rise, Lucas, Soldier of Christ."

Lucas stood, and it seemed his eyes had never seen from such a height. Everything was different now, and his past life held no earthly significance, as he was truly anointed of God. Together they would spread God's word and justice until the final trump sounded. There are thousands of Christian women suffering from Fibromyalgia and, Blessed Bat in hand, Lucas' crusade was just beginning!

MOVING DAY

Silver sat on one of the chairs the movers left positioned within his family room. It had been a very tiring day and it was not over yet. He had a few more things to do before making his bed for a night's rest.

The house was a strange, custom home set in the middle of a quite anomalous, wooded three acres in Huntsville, Alabama. Surrounded by a small stone half-wall with cast iron fence pickets atop, it looked like something more suitable for old New Orleans or homes along a Deep South river. The house itself was Victorian in design, with delightfully complex arrangements of gables and deep porches, but was built in the 1990s rather than the 1890s. Silver had been able to buy the home for very little. Not only were times difficult for those with large mortgages, but the number of such distressed properties had depressed the sale prices to extremely low levels for buyers with cash. Silver was such a buyer.

Walking among all of the boxes and furniture deposited on polished hardwood floors, Silver noticed ample evidence spiders were the dominant inhabitants of the home before his arrival. It was time to do something about that situation.

Sitting down in the middle of the dining room, he called out in a way only an arachnid could fully appreciate: a summons.

After a long minute, a small figure worked its way across the floor towards Silver. It is a Brown Recluse spider, and undoubtedly the closest example of their invertebrate class.

Silver made the overture of a peaceful greeting, which was acknowledged by a waving of the spider's pedipalps.

"I want to speak with your queen," said Silver.

The spider silently regarded Silver, with the equivalent reply of, "what queen?"

"Clearly, my credentials should be presented. I detect that you have a web with two live prey captured within it. Please go and regard your web, returning when you have seen what there is to see," Silver pointed in the direction of the web, flicking a finger minimally.

Silver sat still and waited for the spider's return.

"My prey is dead."

"Yes, it is. They should still be alive should they not?"

"They should."

"Go then once more and see what there is to be seen," Silver said.

Again, Silver sat still and waited.

"More prey has come, bigger."

"Yes, the message is that I can deny or provide. I can promote or eliminate. I prefer to reach an accord. Please summon your queen."

Without comment, the Brown Recluse turned and headed for a nearby baseboard. After a few more minutes, a mouse-sized Wolf spider made its way towards Silver followed by the Brown Recluse.

Standing in front of Silver, the Wolf spider crouched and waited for his words which were not words.

"Your Majesty, the Queen of the Spiders?"

"Yes. Sorcerer you are?"

"Yes. You may address me as Silver."

"What do you want of us?"

"I want lasting peace between us, as this is now my home," Silver said.

"What is peace, as you see it?"

"An absence of conflict, agreed zones to exist, agreed prey, agreed numbers."

"What do we get, from this proposed peace?"

"Safety from the hunt, my goodwill, and food when there is none to be had."

"Details?"

"Absence of conflict, means that I will not war on you or your kind, and your kind will not trouble me or mine. Agreed zones to exist means I want to keep my living areas free of webs or the need to clean them of such. Your portion would be that I will not remove or tamper with webs elsewhere. Agreed prey, any that do not have my parole. I am particularly offended by mosquitoes for example, insects which damage my home or those who I protect are yours. Agreed numbers, control of your population since deaths by misadventure will henceforth be greatly reduced. Safety from the hunt: within the iron fences of my domain, you will not be hunted by anything. My goodwill, for unknown things yet to be considered. Food, when none is to be had, ask your subject there."

"Binding term?"

"Initially, one hundred years. Binding on our descendants?"

"It is either that, move, or die?"

"Yes."

"I agree."

"I agree," Silver said as his hand pushed at an invisible barrier. "As a token of my appreciation I've filled the webs of the webmakers and removed those species of the small whose presence offends me, within my domain."

"May we have two days to ensure full compliance? It will take some time to move where the accord makes necessary."

"Of course." Silver made the parting courtesies that sovereigns do when taking leave of their peers.

Taking a deep breath, Silver walked out onto one of the wide porches. It was a fine autumn day and the trees' leaf color was turning high. Silver sat down in one of the all weather chairs and closed his eyes. His senses detected a number of reptilian species on the property. With a grimace of concentration, he killed all of the snakes where they were. It wouldn't do to simply exile seventy-eight snakes, eighteen of them poisonous, onto his surrounding neighbors. The chipmunks, moles, and voles could simply be given the news of their forced eviction. In his mind's eye, Silver traced wards of limit on the surrounding property lines, which isolated his home from those who travel on the ground. Included in the wards was a provision to request an audience. That provision proved to be in force when a canine mind requested permission to approach. Silver silently granted it.

Coming up the driveway towards the house, came an older woman accompanied by a Golden Retriever named Jezibelle. The woman was carrying a large plastic container.

"I'm up here," Silver called down.

"Hi there, my name is Mercy Hawkins. I live across the street and wanted to welcome you to the neighborhood. I hope you like chocolate chip cookies."

"Hello, Mercy, my name is Silver Brixton. I was just catching my breath out here after seeing the movers off. I love chocolate chip cookies, indeed almost any cookie, but chocolate chip in particular. And who is this? Jezibelle, is it?" Silver said as he courteously extended the back of his hand for inspection by Jezibelle. She took a sniff before giving a quick kiss, tail wagging large.

"How did you know her name? Did I tell you?"

"I can't say. To me she just looked like a Jezibelle. I love dogs, and up to now haven't had the space to provide for one. I expect it will change after I settle in." Silver rubbed Jezibelle's fur and surreptitiously eliminated the fleas, two ticks, and a small mange start. Jezibelle sighed with pleasure. "I'll have to get Jezi's approval for whoever I bring in. Does she go for walks with you? I hear Huntsville has many forest and mountain trails. Perhaps you'll let her walk with me sometimes."

"I do, when my hips aren't acting up and she loves to go. Is Silver your given or a nickname?"

"It's a given name, and I think I got the best deal. My brother's name is Gold and my sister is Platinum. We could go on Oprah for unusual!" Silver motioned Mercy to take a seat. "Now, Mercy, I come from a much more direct society. So I'll now speak to the unasked questions. I'm widowed, without children, of independent means and artistic temperament. I chose Huntsville as my final home due to the availability of this particular house. I find it to be very special." He went on "I'm not a church person, but don't mind people who are. I appreciate a cold alcoholic beverage on occasion. I don't particularly follow football or care about The Crimson Tide, but I will fly the flag on appropriate game days," Silver said and smiled to highlight his goodwill.

Jezibelle leaned heavily into Silver and positioned herself to get a better rub.

"Well, Jezibelle sure likes you. I find that she's generally a very good judge of character," Mercy shook her head in wonder. Gathering herself up, she stood once more "I'll leave you now to the unpacking. If you need anything or have any questions about the neighborhood, just come on over and ask. I'll introduce you to my Ed, he would have come, but he isn't all that mobile anymore. In the spirit of your own disclosures, I think you'll find the neighbors very nice for the most part, and they tend to mind their own business, too. Please bring the container back when you're done with the cookies," Mercy said.

"Thank you, Mercy, I appreciate the welcome and getting to meet the both of you," Silver said.

"Come along, Jezi. You'll see Mr. Brixton again later; he's our new neighbor!"

Jezibelle joined her owner as she headed back down the drive, looking back once with a slow tail wag of farewell.

After they cleared the boundary to the property, Silver said over his shoulder, "You can come out now."

A large female bobcat came out from behind the bush where it had been sitting for the entire encounter, and set about grooming itself on the porch. Silver opened the container and took out a delicious cookie.

"The spiders say there are new rules here," the bobcat said without words.

"Yes. You are welcome to continue living here. In fact, I would enjoy having you. But you would have to agree to the rules of sanctuary. Specifically, you may not kill or hurt any of the creatures I allow within the bounds of my rule. No creatures will kill or pursue you here either. Different rules pertain once outside of the fence, for that is not sanctuary. There will be dogs, but the same rules apply to them."

"I choose to stay. What of my kits when young?"

"They may stay, within limits. We don't need a hundred adult bobcats on our three acres."

The bobcat smiled a toothy, feline smile, "No worries on that front. We prefer to be spread out as adults. But I sense you have access to far more than three acres. How can this be?"

"Very perceptive. Perhaps I'll show you after we are better acquainted. But for now, we'll consider the limits that are immediately apparent." Silver performed a similar service for the bobcat as he had done for Jezibelle. "These grounds will have little to no insect pests, one of the fringe benefits for all of the fur-bearing. You may stay for the next part if you wish. It's time for my discussion with the avian contingent."

"Thank you for the cleansing. Yes, I noticed. I'll just lay down in this patch of sunlight and observe. I think it will be fun to watch."

Silver closed his eyes, and let his senses range the skies. He called the raven, the owl, the hawk, the sparrow, the jay and the hummingbird. Three ravens soon perched on the railing of his porch, strutting back and forth importantly. An owl perched within the shade of a large tree branch. A cloud of twenty sparrows settled noisily in the leaves of the same tree. A jay set down on an inoperative fountain basin. The hummingbird would not land, but hovered. A hawk also set down on the railing, causing brief raven complaints.

"I've called you here to explain the new rules of my home. Your kind will be welcome in moderate numbers, as here there will be no prey or predator. My friend, the bobcat, will not hunt you here. You will not hunt other creatures I have welcomed here. There will be no snakes. Those with nests will not lose their eggs. Outside the fence, the old rules apply. If you don't consider that to be beneficial or the rules to be reasonable, I will banish your kind from my sanctuary. Your decision?" Silver explained and asked.

"Would we be able to nest here?" a sparrow asked.

"Yes, limited numbers for each of your kinds may nest in safety."

The ravens croaked that they agreed, as did all save the owl who alone flew off without making a comment. Silver adjusted the property wards, "The owls will no longer be able to enter these grounds. Welcome to the rest of you and we will speak again."

Silver rose, stretched, and opened the screen door to go back inside. The bobcat followed, looking over the boxes and pieces of furniture spread throughout the house.

Silver smiled, "Please, make yourself comfortable! Might I offer some refreshment?"

"A small bowl of milk would not go amiss, thank you."

Silver raised an eyebrow before opening his refrigerator and pulling out the unopened gallon of whole milk. He poured a cup into a bowl, and heated it slightly with the built-in microwave before setting it down before the bobcat.

"Thank you. Perfectly prepared and very much appreciated. I wonder whether you would also be open to accepting a female mountain lion friend of mine?"

"I would welcome such. Although it would probably be hard to sneak over here, given the location. She would have to agree to not prey on the neighbors' pets, as that could pose a problem. You should probably agree to that as well," Silver said.

"Of course. I'm already well acquainted with Jezibelle, and Mercy who also gives me milk sometimes. Besides it doesn't make sense to hunt so close to where you sleep. My friend would also value a safe place to raise her kittens. It isn't as hard to get here as you might think. The city is well-covered by foliage, and she would be moving at night. One other fringe benefit is that she occasionally provides deer for her friends. Do you like deer?"

"I do. I look forward to meeting your friend." Silver said.

"Thank you again for the warm milk. It takes me back to my days as a kitten. It's also nice to be understood." The bobcat strolled over to the screen door and, standing on her hind legs, used the latch to exit back onto the porch as the sun started to go down.

One final task before he could pack it in for the evening. He took off his shoes and walked out onto the lawn under the largest tree. Communing with flora was much slower than with fauna. Communicating complicated ideas involving boundaries and limits, as well as ways to receive needed help, took Silver several hours of standing stock still. When complete, his trees no longer needed trimming, his lawn mowing, and no weeds would grow within the bounds he had set. This session was much more tiring than the previous ones.

Silver walked back into his house, and found the bobcat had already left for her evening hunt. A raven croaked greeting from above, which Silver reciprocated. The spider webs had already begun to vanish within the house, accumulating instead on the iron fence pickets surrounding the property.

Now, where did I leave that box with my coffeemaker? Silver thought to himself. *It won't do to start tomorrow's work without a fresh cup.*

EXTREME MARKETING

Leo couldn't understand it. He had written two books which should have immediately seen some sales traction on Amazon. They had everything: vampires, werewolves, and witches. He had embedded a heroic quest story arc just as he had been taught while getting his MFA in Creative Writing. One of the books had even been mercilessly workshopped during his college coursework and formed the basis for his final thesis. The MFA cost more than $40K, which he had to borrow since his day job working in a call center would not reimburse any of the expense. But the expense and time was necessary to become a real writer. In Leo's secret thoughts, becoming a real writer was more important than anything else in his life.

Right now he was having trouble even giving the books away! None of his friends would say anything: good, bad or indifferent. He knew his friends weren't spending their $2.99 on the books he had just spent two years writing. How many boxes of girl scout cookies had he purchased over the years to support those so-called friends' children? Shoot, he even offered to provide free books to friends and relatives in exchange for writing a short review on the bookseller website. No takers. Leo didn't care if the reviews said the books sucked; well, he would care but the important thing in the brave new world of online trending was getting ANY reviews.

On Tuesday nights, he went to his writers group. So far, nothing the group had said was paying off. The group had a nominal membership of fifteen people, but usually fewer than ten would show up on any given day. There were three "successful" writers in the group, but now Leo knew there was no way any of them were supporting themselves writing books. Once you saw how Amazon's ratings worked, it was clear that books outside the top 1,000 weren't making any real money. Leo's author ranking bobbed up and down whenever a book was sold, but both titles sat stubbornly around the 2,000,000 mark most of the time - a far cry from 1,000.

This week it was Leo's turn to bring refreshments, so he picked up some chips and dips after work and made his way to Reggie Smoot's home in the hills of Fullerton, California. Reggie's home was worth close to $2 million dollars, mainly because of the stunning views it commanded when the smog wasn't too thick. He was a retired aerospace engineer who took up writing as an activity and seemed to do fairly well, with four published true crime novels, but he certainly didn't depend on it for keep his finances humming.

Normally, Reggie held the meeting outside in the pool patio area, where there was an outside kitchen and countertops to hold refreshments. Reggie spent a lot of time there due to his girlfriend's distaste for smoking inside the house.

Leo would love to be Reggie, even though Reggie was over sixty years old. His girlfriend, Jessica, was significantly younger and carried herself like a model, sometimes she would sit in on the meetings. Leo told himself eventual success would provide similar opportunities, but he sure wasn't going to meet someone like her working in a call center.

Pulling into Reggie's spacious driveway, Leo noticed he was the first arrival. Juggling the refreshments, he pressed the doorbell. He heard steps coming across towards the door and Jessica opened it.

"Hi, Jessica. I'm here for the book club meeting."

"Ah, that explains where Reggie is. Come on in and let's get you unloaded. I think he was setting up a drink station this time." Jessica led the way towards the back patio, her tasteful capris and flats lent a flashback 50s vibe to the home.

Making conversation, Leo spoke up, "Will you be joining the group tonight, Jessica?"

Looking back with a slight smile, Jessica replied, "No. I'm a reader, not a writer. Most of what the group does bores me to tears. I'm better off sitting down and reading something. I'll pop out for refreshments probably. Is there any hummus in that bag?"

"Yes, there is, along with some pita chips."

"Good deal. I'll hand you off to Reggie and go make a sign for the door so I don't have to play butler." Jessica opened the sliding doors to the patio, "Reg, should I leave these open?"

"Yes, please. Hi Leo, how are you doing?" Reggie was in pretty good shape for someone over sixty due to actively running. He looked like the stereotypical aerospace engineer, side-parted gray hair, wearing comfortable long-sleeved shirts with dark slacks which would not have been out of place in a business casual environment. Expensive boat shoes completed the picture.

"I'm a bit frustrated on the writing side of things, but most other aspects are good."

"Alright, let's be sure to address the issues you're having in-meeting. You might not be alone there. Here, let me help you get the refreshments set out. I have some plates and glasses here as well. We're in luck tonight, I had an earlier event and the keg of Bass Ale was barely tapped. Beer lovers rejoice!"

Leo wasn't a huge beer drinker, but he also wasn't paying for the drinks. Working quickly he set the food out as people started to arrive for the night's meeting.

Ramona Sharp, an adjunct professor from a local college arrived with her friend, Lois Gillespie. Both wrote horror novels and short stories, and dressed like Ms. Marple. They were the balance of the successful authors in the group.

Hector Diaz was a young Latino working on a memoir of his childhood and the antics of an especially beloved dog. He also had a day job selling life insurance policies.

Vickie Davenport was a somewhat-fey aging hipster who wrote long-winded fantasy fiction of dreamscapes Leo was sure were chemically-generated. She was also a craft fair stalwart, which couldn't have been too successful either.

The final arrival was Steven Singleton, whom Leo didn't much like. An arrogant, know-it-all graduate student in Cal State Fullerton's creative writing MFA program, he served as editor of the university literary journal. Rather than provide a sense of shared experience, Leo's degree selected him out as someone Steven naturally had to humble. Their two backgrounds were very similar although Steven had yet to hold a real job. He hadn't published anything to date, other than within the journal, although like all MFA students, his thesis would include a novel-length work. Steven was the young hipster in contrast to Vickie, wearing a fedora and up until very recently sporting a neck-beard. Now he had gone back to a well-trimmed goatee.

"Well, it looks like this will be everyone for tonight. Grab some refreshments and let's get started," Reggie said. As the senior member present, Reggie led the group through the normal discussion of writing performed during the last week. Given the disparity in genres, it was interesting to hear the same problems being experienced in different contexts. The accepted procedure was to remain positive and constructive in any comments. Leo thought Steven intentionally made a point of citing esoteric comparisons to display his own erudition more than to help the others. No one else appeared to have their own agenda, so Leo discounted Steven's input as self-serving and moved on.

Once the overview of the prior week's work was complete, the topic changed to more general issues confronting the writers. Reggie nodded at Leo who took it as a cue to bring up the sales problem.

"Group, I am struggling with reconciling the low sales of my two books and the fact I've done my best to incorporate all of the things we've discussed here when it comes to marketing. I've leveraged my personal network, purchased literary reviews (which came back pretty good), paid for advertising on Facebook, paid for advertising on Amazon, offered free copies to reviewers, had price discount promotions, and sponsored contests. Nothing I've done has impacted sales at all. The personal network hasn't even supported doing reviews for free books, on Facebook I get thousands of views but no sales, on Amazon one or two sales were click-related. What am I doing wrong?" Leo asked the group.

"On the ads, what kind of copy is being used?" Steven asked.

"I'm using the back cover blurb the group helped me refine earlier and the cover art. Remember all the early versions needed help?"

"These are fantasy titles, right? How many competitors are out there currently and are there too many new books for the demand?" Vickie asked. "I see a lot of competitors when I put something out, so initial sales to my personal network seems to make all the difference in whether my books are noticed. Facebook hasn't really been money well-spent for me either. It might work with a big enough marketing budget, but I can't afford that."

The group batted more ideas around, but didn't have a magic bullet to help Leo.

"You know, Jessica is a marketing consultant, she might have some ideas we haven't identified. Let me see if she's willing to sit in for a few minutes," Reggie said, rising to find her. A few minutes later, she came back with Reggie, loaded up a plate, grabbed a beverage, and pulled up a chair.

"Reggie has summarized a bit, but it may be helpful for me to hear from everyone on things they do to sell their books," Jessica said.

In turn, each of the published authors detailed the efforts they had made when launching a book. Jessica listened attentively while snacking, nodding her head when it seemed appropriate and asking direct questions. When finished, she turned to Leo.

"Now, Leo, tell me what you've done in your efforts and what kind of results you are seeing."

Leo reiterated his sad tale for Jessica as well.

"OK, I think I see a couple of problems. Everyone here is using what we would call 'spaghetti' marketing. Essentially, you try a bunch of different things at the same time and hope something catches. But those of you who have been successful can't really say which of the campaigns were responsible for your results. In fact, the only thing I am hearing in common is that Facebook advertising doesn't sell books, how do you all know that?"

A babble of voices piped up until Ramona's dominated, "It's because with Facebook, we know how much we spent, we know how many clicks were made, and we know if our sales came from Facebook clicks due to our website analytics."

"OK, so why is everyone paying for Facebook advertising?"

Again a babble erupted. Hector took this one. "Because it is what successful authors do."

"How was that determined and by whom? I'm not trying to be snarky, I want to understand why it is believed."

After further discussion, it becomes clear the authors themselves were repeating things they had heard from other authors. The plethora of online author resources held endless articles posted on the best ways to get noticed. The group had distilled the information into superstition, and did not bring a skeptical mind to evaluate the assertions.

"Is it possible successful authors have no idea which one thing they did to create success? So instead they list all of the things they did without consideration of effectiveness. I see this a lot when working big corporate accounts. Let's start with Facebook. Facebook is a branding tool, not a sales tool. You won't sell much of anything there, despite throwing thousands or millions of dollars out for ads. What you will get is recognition of your name. Now, Leo, no one knows who you are or what you stand for. If you buy enough Facebook ads they will know, but it doesn't mean they will buy your book. This is where they say, 'Leo, yeah I've heard of him but not sure what he does.' Do you think you can afford to spend that kind of money?"

"No, I could barely spend the couple hundred I did. I got a bunch of page likes for my author page, a couple of hundred."

"Are you able to add those people to your personal network?" Jessica asked gently.

"No, I can just see links to their profiles. I could message each one of them I suppose, but Facebook won't make it easy."

"Exactly. Because it's in Facebook's interest to control the interaction themselves. Have you ever looked at the analytic information they provide? It is almost useless if you want to use it for marketing purposes. At my company, we completely ignore Facebook's data and make sure the clicks are recorded on our own website analytics tools so we can know exactly what is happening. Which brings me back to the original question: what would happen if you stopped advertising on Facebook in terms of book sales?"

"Not much, I guess. I haven't sold one book on Facebook."

Jessica clapped her hands, "Now you have money for other things. OK, Leo. If I had to guess I would say you have a breakthrough problem. Even if you've the best book of all time, with the best cover art, the best blurb; if a buyer doesn't see it when they are ready to buy, it won't be successful. How would you buy the latest Dan Brown book? Would you wait until you see an announcement or ad for it, or would you search 'Dan Brown' every so often? How do you make people search for 'Leo'? You could spend several million dollars on a trendy YouTube video with famous celebrities introducing you, you could join the cast of a popular reality show, you could be arrested for a horrendous crime; in short, anything which improved your notoriety for good or ill."

"How does committing a horrendous crime help you sell books?"

Jessica smiled wickedly. "In college, we called it 'Extreme Marketing'. Some of the biggest books by new authors are written by convicts (or ex-politicians) as tell-alls; many people want to read those. Even Hitler's paintings sold better once he was notorious. People read books by serial killers because they want to better understand the mind of a famous serial killer. The theoretical question that arises is: did these people do the deeds to sell their art or to be recognized? Of course, here in California, felons can't benefit from sales of such books."

"That seems sick!" Leo shook his head.

Jessica chuckled at his outrage. "I said it was extreme. But back to you, what can you do to break through? I think for you it will be a matter of personal appeal rather than impersonal, online campaigns. Start attending local book fairs in person with an armful of books. Rather than stand back waiting for someone to ask for a free book, step forward and hand them a copy asking if they would read it. I think you'll find a personal approach will build a quality network over time which eventually results in success. Think of it: a person you don't know steps up to you at a fantasy conference, looks you in the eye and hands you their new book asking only that you read it. Are you going to say no? Of course not! You'll take the book. Will you throw it away? No, it's a book! Will you eventually read it? Probably, because it will sit there calling your name until you do. If it's good won't they tell their friends and search for 'Leo' on Amazon? Isn't that what you are trying to create in the first place? Fans?"

"But it could take years!"

"Yes, it could. But what it won't do is waste much more of your money. The alternative is a hugely wasteful marketing campaign to make you a household name. Do you understand the trade-off as I see it?"

"Leo, your best bet is to go off and kill about twenty people. Then you could enjoy good sales numbers while you sit in jail writing more books," Steven sniped.

Leo laughed along with everyone else, but wondered if Steven had the best advice this time. Of course, Leo would have to think about whether he had the patience to address things slowly, as Jessica suggested. Sitting quietly as the meeting wound down, he couldn't imagine working in a call center for one more year, let alone five to ten. But still, what she said made sense, so he resolved to try the slow approach.

***

In the next three years, Leo wrote five more books while continuing to earn a living in customer care. The book-by-book sales results continued to be lackluster and Leo kept attending book fairs to personally evangelize his growing catalog. During that time, Leo had yet to sell one thousand books. He was also getting tired of the fake smiles of the book fair attendees. Mostly because he realized the book fairs had more authors attending than prospective readers. Clearly this approach wasn't going to work. Besides, a reader goes to a book fair to see an author they already like, rather than find new ones.

Leo stopped attending the writing group shortly after Steven got his first book deal. It was a small publishing house, but it was a deal. Steven was now insufferable in the club meetings instead of being merely unpleasant and Leo no longer looked forward to attending. Jessica and Reggie had parted company, amicably it appeared, so that was one less reason to go. These days, however, Leo had reverted to his introverted self which needed less approval from peers. If you aren't needy, there is little reason to be there, he decided.

Doing some research, Leo found that of the states without a death penalty, Hawaii was the most clement. For some reason, states without a death penalty tended to be in the snow belt. He still hadn't decided to resort to extreme marketing, but he wanted to be in a position to do so. So he resigned his long-standing position at the call center and moved to Hawaii, eventually settling in Maui. He found it simple to lie about having been a waiter in Southern California and was able to land a job where the tips were enough to live modestly but well.

Island time runs differently than its counterpart on the mainland. Leo worked afternoons and evenings, spending mornings writing or snorkeling. In some ways, his life had become close to perfect, but underneath he still had the desire to be recognized for his writing. He could say he was an author, as he had seven published books available for purchase, but like most authors success proved elusive.

One day as he swam chasing brightly colored fish among the off-shore coral, he came to a momentous decision. He would write a book where the protagonist, an unsuccessful writer, plans and executes a series of massacres before being arrested for his crimes. He would make the setting famous Hawaii locations which many were familiar with, right down to the traffic patterns and local color. He would research it meticulously, it would be his first true-crime novel, and as real as possible.

Each day, Leo wrote on his new novel. His small apartment walls were covered with storyboards and plot diagrams. It was his most premeditated novel. Normally, he preferred to start with a general idea and characters then see where it took him. This time everything was MFA-tight: story arc, heroes quest cycle, characterization, and names. The other novels weren't bad, they just didn't step into a formulaic approach. This time Leo would check every box.

Leo hired an editor with money saved a dollar at a time from drunk tourists on vacation. Leo accepted almost all of the recommendations and changes, soon producing a manuscript ready for release. Here, too, he spent liberally for cover art. In the past, he had rushed to publication, feeling every day it wasn't available was a potential loss of sales. This time, he had several proof paperbacks printed and sent them out for paid literary reviews. The process took an extra four months, but at the end he was able to cite all of the big paid reviews in his marketing jacket.

When the book was ready, he released it worldwide all at once. Like the others, it sold a few copies at first then flattened to very few sales. Leo didn't mind, he had other plans.

Lahaina held an annual book fair and festival for an entire weekend and held open special areas for local authors. It was a chance for local readers, tourists, and authors to meet the famous names brought in especially for the occasion. Leo paid for the smallest booth size available, a table really, and ordered several boxes of his books to sell. In the weeks running up to the event, the organizers sent status announcements to all the exhibitors and ran ads on local radio stations. Two weeks before the festival, Leo heard the unimaginable: Steven was on the featured author list for the festival, fresh off of his triumphal 42 weeks in the top ten ranking of the New York Times Best Seller list. Leo had been aware of Steven's success but tried not to let it bother him and definitely did not buy the book! Steven coming in now would ruin everything!

Leo told himself Steven probably wouldn't even know he was there, so it was pointless to stress about it. But resentment and, yes, hatred grew. Leo ran simulations of the conversation they would have if meeting, writing witty comments in advance in case he would have to use them. One way or another, Steven wouldn't be ruining this festival for Leo.

The day came all too quickly and Leo set up his booth which happened to be squeezed between what could only be described as a "Cat Lady" author and a young, nerdy man selling one massive book of sword and sorcery heroic quests plus dragons. *Between these two, my books look like a return to normalcy*, Leo mused.

While sales weren't exactly brisk, he did manage to sell a few autographed books the first day. In each case, the prospective reader was drawn in by the cover art. Surprisingly, the cat lady did very well. Leo guessed having pictures of cats on the covers helped move things along, but he was in too good a mood to snipe. The sullen

Christopher Paolini wannabe selling his dragon epic didn't do nearly as well.

Leo managed to avoid being anywhere near the featured authors group and hadn't laid eyes on Steven. He packed up his stock for the day and looked forward to the next morning.

The second day started much like the first, except this time Leo brought coffee for his neighboring authors. Cat Lady said thanks but she only drank tea, Dragon-Boy insisted that coffee interfered with his meds. *No matter,* Leo thought to himself. *More for me.*

The trio took turns for restroom breaks and covered for each other. Cat Lady sold a book for Leo and handed over precisely the correct amount of cash. He wasn't so lucky when Dragon-Boy was on the job, no sales and several missing books.

Leo put down his irritation with other authors and resolved to enjoy the rest of his time. So far he had sold enough books to cover about 25% of the table fees charged. But he did think a few new fans might have been acquired.

In mid-afternoon, a large crowd of event organizers started touring the tables, presumably bringing the featured authors along.

"Why, if it isn't Leo! Leo and I were part of the same writers group in Southern California," Steven said to an attractive PR functionary at his side. "I guess he is still working the small tables, but let's see what he has for us." Steven hadn't even spoken to Leo, who stood frozen behind the small stacks of his books.

Steven, picked up Leo's latest book, leafed through a few pages before flipping to read the back cover blurb. He set it back down with a derisive snort. "I do like the cover art, good luck!" He turned his back on Leo's booth, "Now, sweetheart, where were we?"

Leo reached down into one of the boxes he had used to bring books.

"Hey, Steven, you asshole! I never did like your covers," Leo shouted.

Steven started and looked back to see Leo holding a MAC-10 aimed directly at him. "Leo, baby, I was just kidding. What are you doing?"

"Extreme marketing, baby!" Leo squeezed the trigger on full automatic for a short burst, jerking Steven's body around before falling to the ground. Leo sprayed the entire entourage of authors and hangers-on in short bursts, before turning back to the Dragon-Boy who he shot once in a leg with his final remaining round. "You'll thank me later."

His shooting complete, Leo placed the gun upon the ground, next to Steven, before lying face-down himself with his arms spread out in front of his booth. As the police arrived, the Cat Lady pointed him out and Leo was arrested forthwith.

***

"Prisoner 01821-089, you have a visitor. Present your hands and follow me," the burly prison guard said. Leo stood up in his cell and held out his arms for the cuffs to be applied then followed.

His lawyer, and agent, Simon Accordi sat waiting with a stack of documents awaiting Leo's signature.

"Hi Simon, how are we doing?"

"Very well, sales are up across the board and proceeds are being placed in the blind trust. The victims' lawsuit is coming along, but I think the movie deal will cover most of the damage."

"Movie deal?"

"Yes, I've been talking to a studio interested in a movie covering the events leading up to the shooting. I've promised them your full cooperation on the script which is why they are considering top dollar. Of course, the proceeds have to go to the victims."

"Of course. How is Dragon-Boy doing?"

"Excellent, his leg healed fine and his books have never sold better. He was just picked up by a major. How are things going for you in here?"

"Not too bad, I've lots of time to write. I'll have another novel for you in two months. Also, you'd be surprised how many of these guys want to write a book about themselves. I've got a few people I'm helping right now, we might want to do something there in about a year."

"Very good. I'll be off, don't hesitate to call if you need something."

"I won't," Leo said.

In twenty five years, when eligible for parole, he'd have a formidable catalog and still only be in his mid-fifties. Not bad! Time enough to build an empire.

BROUGHT TO YOU BY

Bryan sat in the sterile brightness of the waiting room at Evergreen Urology Center, reading the usual array of uninteresting magazines you find in a doctor's office. Each magazine had a small label with Dr. Simonton's name and what was presumably his home address. *Really bad idea*, Bryan thought to himself. *I wonder why he just didn't use the office address? Perhaps he doesn't have any unhappy clients.*

In addition to dog-eared periodicals, there was a shiny display of procedure brochures as well. Looking around the room to make sure no one else was paying attention, Bryan picked up several purporting to deal with erectile dysfunction. You could tell which ones without even reading the pamphlet titles, they featured smiling, older, heterosexual couples, with the women appearing particularly pleased. Reading the titles wouldn't have helped much anyway since they were all devoted to meaningless marketing brand names. The center even had a few, presumably named after the clinic itself: "Everlastic", "Everest", and "Everfirm".

As usual with such marketing material, the details a person like Bryan would want to know were not included.

Bryan wanted to fully understand a procedure's process: how long it took, what recovery period was required, what side effects were possible, and how often those side effects occurred. But most important of all, how much did it cost? None of those details were provided, the brochures threw general terms like "affordable", "minimal side-effects", and "well tolerated" around as though they actually meant something objective. Bryan wanted to decide those things for himself and would need better data in order to do so.

"Mr. Stillman?" a young woman wearing scrubs called from the doorway.

"That's me," Bryan said gathering his things to follow her into an examination room.

"My name's Allison, I'll be taking your information before Doctor Simonton sees you. First, let's get your vitals."

Allison took Bryan's temperature, recorded blood pressure and heart rate before having him step on a scale for weighing. Bryan followed her directions through the normal process.

"Everything looks good, so what brings you to the Center?"

Bryan took a deep breath and decided to just come out with it. Normally, this wasn't something he would confess to any woman, but he was here needing help and hopefully she was as professional as appearances suggested.

"As I've gotten older, I'm having more trouble maintaining an erection when having sex with a partner. The initial onset is pretty normal, but if the sex isn't continually exciting, the erection falls quickly. It's like the blood has better things to do and goes to do them."

Allison smiled at the last statement, "That isn't uncommon as men age. Do you have trouble with ejaculation?"

"Not really. It isn't as powerful as when I was younger, but it happens just fine as long as my penis stays erect." Bryan found it easier to speak as the conversation progressed. "I know things still work, as masturbation doesn't seem to have the same issue. Of course, there I pretty much get things done directly without diversion. I don't do that with a partner, there are periods with less stimulation when I'm focused on her, but before I could mostly maintain an erection throughout."

"Have you tried any of the medicinal approaches, like Viagra or Cialis?" Allison asked.

"Yes, they worked only periodically, and the side-effects were off-putting. I'm one of those people who flush in the face and neck when using the product. I look like a beet! My girlfriend thought I was having a heart attack which killed the mood most times."

"When was the last time your prostate was checked?"

"My last yearly physical, it's enlarged but normal. The PSA values were also in the normal range."

"So, in summary, you're here to explore solutions to maintain an erection throughout your sexual encounters?"

"Yes. Of course, I would prefer for any such solution to not cause other problems fixing that one," Bryan clarified.

"Noted. Doctor Simonton will come in after he has a chance to read your chart, perhaps fifteen minutes. Would you like some water or juice while waiting?"

"No, thank you. I'm fine."

Allison nodded and left the examining room. Bryan looked around and discovered another rack with magazines. Bypassing that, he perused the medical illustration posters of the Urologist's stock in trade adorning the walls. A brochure rack held paeans to Cialis, Viagra, and other similar procedures.

A few minutes after Bryan had given up his quest for waiting room entertainment, Dr. Simonton knocked on the door and entered. A man younger than Bryan, wearing a fitted, long-sleeved shirt and skinny jeans appeared carrying a tablet computer. A thick gold chain resting atop a tuft of thick chest hair completed the picture.

This guy looks like he is ready to hit a disco instead of work, Bryan thought. *Hope he knows his business.*

"Mr. Stillman? I'm Dr. Simonton. What brings you in today?"

Bryan shook his head internally, but dutifully reiterated what he had already told Allison. Dr. Simonton made notes and attentive noises as he listened to Bryan's tale.

"A question, Bryan. Has this been an issue with more than one partner?" Dr. Simonton asked.

"Yes. I thought at first my problem was due to boredom or something since I had been with my girlfriend for more than ten years. But it wasn't that. I had the same problem eventually with others. Anytime I slow things down it seems to happen."

"OK. I see you don't like the drug options, due to flushing? Yes, that can be a problem, making the wrong head flushed." Dr. Simonton scanned Bryan's face for a reaction to the small joke, found none, and moved on without further attempts at humor.

"Bryan, we have several options. I recommend either of our Everfirm or Everlastic procedures. Everfirm is a surgical solution which delivers an always semi-tumescent condition for the penis. It still will enlarge further when aroused, but doesn't ever shrink down to a fully deflated state. Some men like it because the penis is always noticeable even when not erect."

"Wouldn't that cause a problem wearing underwear and clothing?"

"You would have to purchase larger underwear to be comfortable, as well as placing things properly when putting on the rest of your clothes."

"What about wearing a swim suit?"

"It would be noticeable no matter how cold the water. Again, the men who prefer this like it due to never again having shrinkage. I have a couple of uncles I've treated using this approach."

"I don't know, I'm not as concerned about how things look in public. I just want it to work properly in private."

"Very well, it sounds like you might want the Everlastic procedure instead. In this one, things will regain whatever facility you had when younger, with one exception. Your penis will be under your conscious control; it will erect when desired and remain erect until you decide it is time to finish up."

"You mean I will give it orders?" Bryan asked. "How does that work?"

"There are two processes, first to physically repair the structures to their youthful condition and finally to impart a deep neural conditioning tied to an agreed mental signature. Basically, we'll agree on the words or commands then I'll program it into your limbic system. You'll use a code word to maintain an erection and a code word to release it."

"What about ejaculation, does it affect things?"

"Depending on your normal arousal process, you'll ejaculate but your penis will continue to stay erect until mentally released."

"Wow! Really? And everything feels the same?"

"Yes, only more so as being multi-orgasmic is possible whenever you want it. Just know your own limits, as we had one gentleman die after going through several days of sex without eating or resting. He never activated the release and his penis had to be drained before he could be buried. He died happy, I suppose."

Bryan winced at the mention of draining. "Ouch! But I guess he wasn't alive to feel it. I doubt I will have the same problem. Everlastic sounds right for me, what are the next steps?"

"The physical procedure requires general anesthesia as we can't have movement when performing the microsurgery. You'll be in the hospital two days afterwards, and also have to take it easy for another 30 days to finish healing. No sex until the healing is complete. The neural conditioning is done twice a week during the healing period. After that you should be good-to-go."

"When can I get it done?"

"Well, we have to talk about payment. The procedure is pretty expensive, and your insurance doesn't cover it. All in, we're talking about $50,000 total." Dr. Simonton looked expectantly at Bryan.

"$50,000! I don't have that kind of money. Why doesn't insurance cover it?"

"They see it as an elective procedure. A man's sexual health isn't important enough to be considered necessary. You could get a sex change operation and it would be fully covered, but not anything considered solely a male issue. Insurance companies don't see your erection as necessary. If you were trying to conceive a child, they would pay for extraction of the sperm rather fixing a problematic erection with surgery," Dr. Simonton explained. "I'm fairly certain Everlastic would work for you. Did you want to speak with my practice manager to explore options?"

"Yes. I'm not going to be able to get my life on track without sorting this out."

"I look forward to helping you with that. Good day, Mr. Stillman. It was a pleasure to meet you. I'll have Betty come in shortly to go over the options." Dr. Simonton left after shaking Bryan's hand.

It was only a few more minutes before an older woman came in. "Mr. Stillman, I'm Betty. Please come with me to my office so we can free up the examination room. Besides, it's more comfortable." Betty smiled amiably. Bryan followed her into a well-appointed office with a traditional wooden desk set. Betty sat down behind the desk and indicated Bryan should sit in one of the comfortable leather chairs arrayed in front.

"Dr. Simonton mentioned your interest in our Everlastic procedure. Truly, many patients before you have found their results to be life-changing. He also mentioned a need for alternate financing. Let's talk through what we can do for you."

Bryan and Betty went through the usual financial information. He didn't have a lot of ready cash available, and his credit cards were already at the upper end of their limits. His income as a credit union manager wasn't enough to secure an outright loan for the surgery.

"Bryan, I'm really sorry. There doesn't appear to be any way this operation can be directly financed, given your situation," Betty said regretfully.

Bryan's face fell, as he had been hoping for a miracle on more than one front. "Isn't there anything you can do?" he asked.

After a moment's reflection, Betty said, "There may be something, but I will have to look into it over the next few days. Do you have social media profiles available for reference? I'll use them for my discussions with a few third parties."

"Sure, everyone has a presence these days," Bryan said and wrote down the profile links for his various services then handed them to Betty.

"Thank you! My, you are well-represented! I've found that to be helpful when discussing financing with these sources. Thank you for your time; I'll do my best to put something together in the next few days." Betty stood, signaling the meeting was over. She walked him through the lobby and held the door, waving as he left the practice.

Bryan went home and spent the next few days obsessing on ways to get his hands on $50,000. One thing he hadn't mentioned to the doctor was that his most recent girlfriend had left him, fed up with his inability to keep things going in the bedroom. Given the bruising his ego had taken upon her exit, he wasn't prepared to engage again until he could be reasonably sure the penis was working properly. Bryan was an extremely social creature, though, he loved being in a relationship and being alone was not for him. So he spent time online flirting with several women he was interested in, making sure to never take it to the next level. When asked, he said he had some family issues to work through, which was usually enough to keep things on simmer.

When the phone rang a few days later and the caller ID said "Evergreen Urology", he scrambled to pick up the call.

"Hello?"

"Mr. Stillman? This is Betty from the Evergreen Urology Center, I have some wonderful news for you. I think we have a way to do the Everlastic procedure if you can find $5,000. The rest would be covered by a sponsor who supports Dr. Simonton. How does that sound?"

There was silence while Bryan quickly ran the math in his head on where he could find $5,000. If he took all of his cash and charged the balance across three credit cards it would work! "It sounds great! I can use separate credit cards to get the balance?" Bryan asked eagerly.

"We can definitely do that. When did you want to have the procedure? We have to arrange for a hospital stay of three to four days," Betty said as she worked with Bryan to get the next available spot on the surgery schedule.

***

The day of Bryan's operation came all too quickly, he took a week of vacation and arrived at the surgery center. Betty met him in the lobby carrying a large envelope of paperwork.

"Let's go to my office and get these completed. Lots of forms here for you to sign!" Brian followed her back and was soon signing every document she placed in front of him. He handed Betty his cash and credit cards so she could process his portion of the payment.

Bryan read over the forms. Most were variations of things he had seen many times in the past: health history and vitals, privacy forms, and a thick binder titled "Evergreen Sponsorship Agreement". He assumed it covered the $45,000 he was being granted, but the language was so convoluted as to be impenetrable. Filled with phrases like "Party of the first part", "Party of the third part", using terms like "subrogation" and "force majeure". What the hell, he couldn't understand any of it. He saw the $45,000 mentioned as part of something else indecipherable. Setting the agreement aside, he worked through the other forms he mostly understood and waited for Betty's return. After a few more minutes she returned, handing Bryan a receipt for his records.

"Betty, a quick question. I can't make heads or tails out of the sponsorship agreement, what is it for?"

"It sets forth the terms under which the sponsor has provided funds for your procedure. Mostly it protects the sponsor should something go wrong with the surgery, but also provides for the Center to report on the results of the surgery. The surgery procedure is still new and presenting papers or videos of a successful procedure will help the sponsor and clinic acquire new patients," Betty explained.

"Seems like a very complex document if that it is meant to do," Bryan said.

"You are welcome to consult an attorney, if you wish. I don't know the nuts and bolts myself. If you want to do that before signing, we'll need to cancel today's procedure and reschedule for after the agreement is completed."

Bryan thought through the options; delay would mean a revised vacation schedule with the bank, which they would not appreciate. The cost of a lawyer hadn't been considered and he didn't have any money left to pay one. *How bad could it be?* he said to himself. *Just sign the damn thing and move on!*

"I'll sign it now, no need to delay matters," Bryan said and used his pen to make the necessary entries.

Betty gathered all of the paperwork into a folder labeled with Bryan's name. "Very good! I'll walk you over to the surgery check-in."

She handed Bryan off to a surgical nurse wearing scrubs and left.

Bryan stowed his clothes and possessions inside the assigned locker and sat on the examination table wearing backless hospital garb. Dr. Simonton walked in a few minutes later wearing surgical garb.

"Bryan, have you decided on the key words to actuate and deflate?"

"One question, do I have to say the word aloud for it to be effective?"

"No, just thinking about it will work. Remember, it isn't just saying the word, it should be paired with the image of an erection to be effective. We will create the linkage during surgery. The word itself can be used otherwise without effect as long as you don't pair it with the image. The same goes with the deflate command."

"OK, I don't want it to be something I use ordinarily so I've decided on "Montezuma" for erection and "Tripoli" for deflation."

"Nice! Semper Fi! Those will work well and be hard to forget also. I'm going to have the anesthesiologist come in to get you ready for us. I'll see you after the surgery to go over how it went."

In minutes, Bryan lay sedated on a gurney with multiple IVs as he was wheeled into the operating room.

****

Bryan woke up in a recovery room with a feeling of dull numbness in his groin as the painkillers continued to do their work. A nurse came in with a cold orange juice, which tasted better than any had for a long while.

"How long was I in surgery?"

"Seven or eight hours. It's extremely complex microsurgery. Dr. Simonton always looks like he has run a marathon after doing one of these," the nurse said.

"How did it go?" Bryan knew the nurses probably weren't permitted to steal the doctor's thunder, but gave it a shot anyway since he was eager to know.

"The doctor will be in shortly to discuss it."

Dr. Simonton came in and he did look tired. He stood next to the examination table which had been raised to a sitting position for Bryan's recovery.

"Bryan, everything went great in surgery, no surprises. We'll keep you in the hospital for two days while you're wearing a catheter just to be extra careful. Anytime you do a surgery it pays to observe how things go during recovery. Important: do not use your command word while wearing the catheter, it would be painful. Otherwise, in the meantime, relax and get some rest. In two weeks everything will be working better than ever. Here is your folder of instructions, stick to it and I doubt you will need my services ever again." Dr. Simonton added a few more pleasantries and left.

Bryan found he was more tired than he knew once he got to his hospital room. He was sharing with a talkative retiree who had the Everfirm procedure several days earlier and was scheduled for release the next morning. Bryan fell asleep listening to how much his roommate was going to enjoy the expressions on the ladies' faces when he went swimming at the retirement center.

Two days later, Bryan was released. He went home and very quickly was back into his usual routine. He continued flirting online with a couple of women, anticipating being able to get back into the swing of things very soon. At work, compliments were offered on how he seemed to be more positive and the vacation must have worked. He smiled, thanked them, but told no one of his surgery.

The day finally came when Bryan was able to take the wraps off of his new working penis. He tested it by masturbating to some of his favorite porn. Everything felt and worked great, just like it did when he was in his twenties! It was time to take his relationship with one of the online contacts to the next level. Happily, Byran logged onto the hookup site to arrange for some company for dinner and afterward.

A woman named Susan proved amenable to his charms and agreed to meet him at the restaurant. Bryan dressed for the occasion, with slacks and shirt he knew he looked good in. Waiting at the bar, he watched the door in anticipation. Susan walked in only five minutes late wearing a tight pencil skirt and silk blouse combination - she looked stunning. Bryan waved from the bar.

"Hello, Bryan?" she asked.

"Yes, hi! You look great! Did you want to get a cocktail prior to dinner, or get seated?"

"I'm hungry, so it would be good to get seated. I can get a drink with dinner. Bryan, you look much better than your profile picture."

"Thank you, things have been going well for me lately and maybe it shows. I heard this place has great prime rib and the wine selection is supposed to be pretty good, too."

"Great! Let's get seated."

Before Bryan knew what happened, he was telling self-deprecating stories about his banking position and being impressed by her career as a paralegal. One wine bottle became two, one thing followed another, and they wound up in Bryan's bed quicker than he had dreamed. Everything worked perfectly, Bryan had released after ejaculating so as not to appear odd. It was clear Susan was ready for round two, when she ducked under the covers. Bryan grinned and thought "Montezuma" to himself, picturing a robust example of his own erection. There was a squawk of surprise and Susan's head came out from under the covers.

"What the heck is going on, your penis is glowing!" Susan said.

"Whaaa?" Bryan looked down, and could barely make out letters glowing on the surface of his penis. "What does it say?"

Susan laughed, "It says 'This Erection Brought to You by Evergreen Urology'. Did you get their special sponsor's package?"

Feeling stupid suddenly, Bryan said "How do you know about that?"

Susan laid back on Bryan's bed, "Hey, if we're going to talk you might want to turn that thing off." Bryan thought "Tripoli" with the requisite image and down it went.

"OK, so I had a bit of work done myself, at Evergreen Cosmetic Surgery. I couldn't afford to pay for all of it myself so I signed their sponsorship contract. I'll bet the two are part of the same group."

"I didn't see anything glowing on you, where is your sign?" Bryan ran his fingertips across her smooth waist onto her hips.

"Since you asked me nice, I'll show you. Crank that bad boy up again." Turning over onto her hands and knees, she turned back and asked, "Do you like tattoos?"

Chuckling, and once more ready for action, Bryan said, "Doesn't everyone?"

"Grab my butt cheeks at the same time"

Bryan did this thing and gasped. Susan's back became a kaleidoscope of colors as the tattoo of a dragon appeared, along with artfully displayed message saying "Brought to you by Evergreen Cosmetic".

"Twist the right cheek clockwise, you don't have to force it."

Bryan gasped as the images changed with each toggle of the cheek. "Amazing!" Settling upon a glorious rendering of a tramp stamp, his hands rose once more to her waist and soon both lost their power of speech.

Bryan's phone began buzzing as message after message arrived. Messages from friends, relatives, co-workers all asking variants of the same question, "What the hell are you doing dude? Livestreaming your sexual encounters on social media!"

Bryan paid no attention to the messages until several hours later when Susan and he came up for air. He read all of them while preparing some refreshments in his kitchen. Susan sat at the coffee table wearing one of his shirts.

"This is weird, all of my friends are telling me our lovemaking was broadcast onto my social media. I wonder how that happened?"

"Yes, it's a shock at first, but you get used to it. Welcome to the Evergreen Reality Show. The first thing you will want to do is change your privacy settings so the feed won't automatically be shown to your friends," Susan said matter-of-factly.

"Feed, what feed?"

"Camera and microphone feed, silly. If yours is like mine, there are small cameras installed where the work was done, and they uplink automatically when the modifications are activated. So viewers got to see your face riding me home on my feed, while yours was probably showing something much more graphic. The show puts all the streams together and curates the best for broadcast.

It's breaking all the records for audience. Go ahead, check your social media."

Bryan opened the app and immediately saw a string of posts on his account which had been pulled down by the provider. They hadn't eliminated all of the comments from his friends and acquaintances made during or shortly after his lovemaking episode. Bryan sat in shock, and quickly changed his settings to limit exposure.

"How much are we obligated to share? By the contract I mean, I don't have the cash to hire a lawyer to explain it to me."

"Your days of cash worries are probably over, Bryan. Here, look, our segments aired to a worldwide audience of 25.2 million, calculated at the big finish. We were especially big in Korea, coinciding with their lunchtime. Most of my viewers come from there, but together we pulled bigger numbers than usual, so they like you. Evergreen sends royalties depending on market share, so you probably made more money on our evening than you did at work. As for the contract, it is pretty airtight. You accepted a sponsorship deal and are locked in for the contract term."

"But I didn't understand what I was signing. Can't I get out of it?"

"Unfortunately, if you can read and aren't mentally deficient, that isn't a way out. Were you coerced?" Susan laughed as she was clearly enjoying Bryan's reactions. "You'll be able to hire a lawyer when your royalties come in, or you can enjoy yourself. Think of it this way: if you had a NASCAR team and signed a sponsorship agreement, you would expect to race under their logo, wouldn't you?"

"Yes, but this goes way beyond that! I mean, broadcasting worldwide, people I don't even know watching my intimate moments. How could I go outside?"

"I know; paparazzi and fans can be off-putting. Unless you make a big deal, though, most of the time they wouldn't know you from anyone else. In my case, the back camera array doesn't catch my face. It would have caught you making any crazy sex faces, though. Your body camera, if I am not mistaken, is installed in the head of your penis. Viewers, in essence, get to be your penis." Susan patted Bryan's shoulder, "You're a nice guy, Bryan. Give it some time before you decide this was a bad idea."

Bryan clasped her hand in thanks. "How much money can you make on this?"

"I like my day job, and I want to keep it for the time when this is all over. But in my case, I make close to three times as much with the royalties. Pretty good for just continuing to live life. I'm banking the royalties for the most part. Fads move pretty fast, so this won't always be here. This footage helps build the audience as well. They always like the reveal when newbies are brought on board." Susan pointed out the cameras installed in Bryan's kitchen and apartment.

Finally finding the situation amusing, Bryan laughed. "This changes everything; the Kardashians are finished, and not a moment too soon!"

"That's the spirit!"

Montezuma!

THE ROSETTA LOCI

Being low on the totem pole, Annie Richardson didn't rate an assistant or even the sharing of one. She opened her office mail quickly so as to get through the disagreeable task as soon as possible. As a newly-frocked Associate Professor of Linguistics, her joy for landing the rare position was tempered by the realization her department would be expecting a research proposal in short order. She had been so focused on getting the job that her next steps were not so well-defined. In Annie's well-ordered mind, there was little point in planning for something which wouldn't be needed should the job fall through. She also knew that coming up with suitable projects would not be difficult.

Most of the dwindling mail pile represented various directives from the university concerning the upcoming term. Teaching undergraduates entry-level linguistics was something she could do in her sleep, but the university defined guidelines and expected everyone to comply. Annie set those aside in a separate pile for later processing.

A large, heavy envelope embossed with the world-recognizable logo of Western Sensing, Inc. was next in line. *What the heck? Who is it addressed to?* Annie looked over the address label, half-expecting it to be addressed to "occupant" or perhaps the prior tenant of her cramped office in the Social Sciences building. But no, it was addressed to Dr. A. Richardson. Curiosity piqued, Annie slid her finger into the flap and tore it open.

Inside, accompanying what was clearly a product brochure, was a letter requesting her presence at a demonstration of the Insight 2500 sensing module, a part of their premier bio-sensing line of products. The letter complimented her thesis "Physiological Basis of the Brain Encoding of Human Language" and stated the demonstration would present a modality which would allow for empirical proof of her theories. The demonstration would be followed by dinner according to the ticket which was also included.

Wonderful! Even if it is the bee's knees, there is no way my budget would support buying one of those damn platforms. They are about the same price as a supercomputer, and no one is lining up to give me that kind of funding. Shoot, I'm lucky to make payments on my student debt! But I would love to see what this device can do. And a free meal in the bargain? I'm so there!

Annie marked her calendar and pinned the ticket to her bulletin board for easy access. The next few weeks passed and she had almost forgotten about the event when her phone rang. The wired telephone in her office was definitely a throwback to the days when mobile phones weren't available. Normally, she would just let it ring through. Today, for whatever reason, she picked up. Anything was better than grading another vapid exam blue-book.

"Hello, Professor Richardson?" an anonymous male voice asked.

"This is she, who is calling?"

"I'm sorry, I should have said. Starting over! I'm Fidel Munos and I work with Western Sensing. I'm calling to urge your attendance for the Insight 2500 demonstration and dinner tomorrow night. Were you planning to come?" Fidel asked.

"I forgot all about it, so I guess it's good that you called. I was planning to come, just out of interest, and the prospect of a good meal. Tell me, sir, will there be a good meal?" She asked playfully.

Fidel laughed wholeheartedly, "I told the organizer there would be better participation if a meal was included. I remember the post-thesis famine myself."

"Really, you're a linguist as well?"

"No, an unholy mixture of physiological psychology and artificial intelligence, I'm afraid."

"That is an unholy mix! I am planning to come but I have to state up front we don't have much in the way of research funding here. As much as I suspect I'll love the capabilities, I doubt my department head will see anything other than a budget breaker," Annie cautioned.

"You might be surprised. The capabilities are rather in excess of what the company expected, which is why we're reaching out to various interested parties. Try to evaluate the potential without concern for the cost, if you can do so."

"Fidel, you work for Western Sensing? What do you do there?"

"Research in my line of interest. They hired me away from MIT four months ago. Believe it or not, even MIT doesn't have the funding for every project."

"OK, now I'm intrigued. Excuse my asking, but what is the dress code?"

"No worries, business casual is fine. I'm sure there will be folks on either end of the spectrum, though. I'll mark you down as a yes, and I hope to meet you in person."

Annie said goodbye and went back to grading students' work.

***

The next day went by in a whirl. Classes were perfunctory and office hours short on specious dolts. At 4 p.m. Annie closed and locked her office door, heading home to change before catching the subway to the Western Sensing building. She'd decided on the serious academician look: a pair of dress slacks, a jacket, and sensible flat shoes.

Following the signs from the lobby, she walked up to three badge tables set up according to ranges of the alphabet. She approached the one labeled "R-Z" and announced herself.

"Annette Richardson? Please show me your Driver's License or other ID," a pleasant but firm woman said, clutching a clipboard full of names.

"Certainly, here it is," Annie held it out for the woman's inspection.

The woman's voice became markedly more friendly, "I'm sorry for the hassle, Dr. Richardson. We've had several representatives from the media trying to get in using other's credentials, so we're being extra careful. Here's your badge, and we have a small souvenir bag for you as well. I'll take your ticket now, and you can join the others outside the conference hall for cocktails and snacks. The presentation begins at 7 p.m. If you have any questions or need anything, come see me or one of the others here. Have a great time!"

Annie thanked her and wandered around the curve into a huge open space where people stood wearing badges and sipping cocktails. The total number appeared to be more than one hundred. It had the look of a faculty cocktail party set in a better venue.

Being a staunch introvert, Annie made her way to one of the convenient bars set up outside the conference hall and ordered a glass of wine. Unlike faculty parties, it was delivered in a glass rather than a plastic cup. Taking a sip, she stood back and watched the others.

A handsome young man with a slight Hispanic look came bustling back, stopping short when he saw Annie's nametag.

"Professor Richardson! Hello, I'm Fidel, we spoke on the phone yesterday. I'm glad to see you made it," he said as he held out a hand.

Struggling to balance her drink and bag, she set the bag down and shook his hand. "I remember," Annie said smiling, "You're responsible for my presence, as I certainly would have forgotten the presentation without a reminder."

Fidel laughed, "You're not alone in that! Precisely why I made the calls. Do you prefer to be addressed as Professor or Doctor?"

"'Annie' works just fine as long as you're properly respectful. How about you, Doctor?"

"How could I be anything other than 'Fidel' now?" They laughed together.

"Listen, I have a few things to do before the presentation kicks off, but would you like to sit with me?" Fidel asked.

Annie flushed before tamping it back, "Sure, are they going to call us in with an announcement?"

"Yes, I'll be making it along with a few others. Why don't we meet back here a couple of minutes before 7?"

"Sounds good."

Fidel hurried off at much the same speed with which he had entered.

Annie went back to watching the room and its occupants while sipping at the wine.

***

As promised, just before 7 p.m. Fidel and several other people walked through the crowd announcing the start of the presentation. The crowd began to work their way through the multiple entry doors. Inside, the room was appointed much like an auditorium, seats in rows descending in level to a stage in the front. The chair fittings were much more comfortable than the standard hard chairs at the university. Fidel met her at the appointed spot and escorted her in. Picking a row midway down the aisle, he guided her to two chairs in the middle.

Fidel smiled at her. "I'm glad you agreed to sit with me. I've read your thesis myself and want to speak more with you about it after you've seen what the sensing module can do,"

Annie shifted in her seat, pleased with attention but unaccustomed to it. "Even my thesis examiners had trouble staying awake after reading it, and they were paid to do so! What interests you about it?"

"My interest is the brain and how it encodes information, from an AI perspective. I promise to bore you with the details at dinner, if you'll sit with me. Right now they're kicking things off."

Now it was Annie's turn to laugh, "Alright." It wasn't often men sought Annie out for dinner conversation. It wasn't a lack of attractiveness, but men tended to find her abrupt and unashamedly intelligent. Too much so for most tastes.

The lights dimmed and the founder of Western Sensing, Warren Dawes, strode onto the stage lit by a spotlight.

"Distinguished guests, welcome to our presentation! Each of you has contributed to study of the problem of how humans and, indeed, life itself encodes and uses information. Up until now, we haven't been able to look inside the box of fragile organic systems without damaging or destroying the object of study. That changes tonight with the Insight 2500," Dawes dramatically gestured as lights hit what was presumably an Insight 2500 installation. "I know many of you have been concerned about cost, and I urge everyone to put that aside for the time being. We have a different proposition to make. For now, I'll hand off it to our Vice President of Product Development for a rundown on what the Insight 2500 can do."

A perfectly-coiffed woman stepped up and started the demonstration. Annie's interest was captured immediately when she learned the device could capture and record the firing patterns of individual neurons in the brain, without surgery, contrast dyes, or other impediments to the subject. Furthermore, the device could also stimulate a specific neuron or neurons to fire. Just those two capabilities represented a huge leg-up on being able to empirically test Annie's theories. So many things she could do! Her mind manically raced from one idea to the next. Fidel had been watching her involuntary facial expressions transit her face. He chuckled briefly, nodded his head then smiled and motioned towards the presentation when she looked over at him.

The rest of Western Sensing's guests were similarly impressed. Each had a special theory or research question the Insight 2500 would enable testing. Finally, the presentation was over and a cacophony of voices rose up when the call for questions came. Most were a variant of "How can we believe this is real?" and "How do we get to use the Insight 2500?" For the latter, the charismatic Warren Dawes stepped forward once more.

"We plan to operate an Insight 2500-equipped lab in every major city represented by the persons invited. We will bear the entire cost of operation, maintenance, and of course the initial investment. We'll negotiate agreements with interested parties to use the system. Some of you will be offered employment within Western Sensing, others will receive grants to fund your portion of the research. We will, of course, participate financially in any discoveries which come out of our joint efforts."

Ah, here we go, the strings which come with the deal! Annie thought to herself.

Dawes continued, "We expect all of you to prime our pump, so to speak. The research papers you publish will drive sales of the next generation of Insight equipment and services. Your peers will be envious and want to participate, however, only the first adopters will be granted such favorable terms. In the next few weeks, we'll reach out to each of you to ascertain interest in our proposal and negotiate an agreement. For tonight, the only thing left on the agenda is dinner." He waved grandly and left the stage.

With that, the lights came up and more than one hundred people began talking excitedly among themselves as they filed into what proved to be an immense dining room. Seated next to Fidel, Annie enjoyed more wine and one of the best chicken piccata meals she had ever been served.

"What do you plan to investigate first, Annie?" Fidel asked.

"I'm thinking I should start small. Probably by lining up some subjects to show pictures to and have them say aloud what the picture depicts. Simple objects. It would be great to see which nerves are involved and look for commonalities between subjects. Then we can do the same thing with people who don't speak English. I mean just those two things would yield a lifetime of research papers! I'm going to have to think hard on it to decide…there are way too many options here. How about you, Fidel, what are you chasing, if you don't mind my asking?"

"Not at all. I have a particular site in the brain I want to investigate. It is a small nexus of nerve cells without a known purpose. Where it's situated suggests a relation to sight, semantics, and language. I might have to tap your expertise as we go if the last proves to be true. I plan to selectively stimulate the neurons and ask subjects what they perceive is happening. It may be a dry hole and subjects might not even be aware of the stimulation, but I won't know until I try it. If I can figure this out, they might have a reason to name it Munos' Loci," Fidel laughed.

"Ambitious! Me, I would simply like to get some answers before hitting retirement age. So much of what we have done in the past is evolved theory because direct experimentation was not possible. Insight changes everything! I am so happy you picked up the phone and called," Annie was not generally so effusive, but the night's news, food, and good company had conspired to make her expansive.

"I wish I could take full credit for it, but as you can tell from my research plans, having a linguist in the mix will only improve my chances. Are you open to joining Western Sensing, or would you prefer to continue your association with the university?"

"I'm not immediately sure. One huge advantage of staying at the university is the platform for publishing research papers, but it comes with the need to coddle undergraduates at the same time. How do you handle the research paper issue with Western owning the intellectual property?"

"I'm more interested in getting to the truth, plus having my name on a human body part. All joking aside, though, they do own the lion's share of the IP. Unlike the traditional corporate model, I actually own a minority share. If I discover something useful, I'll make millions. In the old days, they would hand the inventor/scientist a couple hundred dollars, a nice plaque commemorating the achievement, and that's it. I should know, my dad has a ton of those on his home office wall and only has his pension to live on."

"Wow, really? How do you publish?"

"It works the same as it does within academia," he explained, sipping his wine. "Instead of an internal department committee deciding, I run it through our IP lawyers before submitting it to journals. By necessity, we keep important things to ourselves, but other, more broad, elements are shared so interested third parties can peer review and validate. In our case, it also drives sales of Insight equipment, because our studies can't be replicated without it."

"It comes back to selling equipment, doesn't it?" Annie asked, an edge of disappointment creeping into her voice.

Fidel wobbled his hand. "Yes and no. When you create a new capability, money is made both on the equipment and what the equipment makes possible. I guarantee you Dawes isn't focused solely on the equipment. I suspect he would give it away at cost if he had to. This whole situation is unique to both science and technology; it requires a new way to take full advantage, hence the good treatment of the help. I'm looking forward to buying my first beach house," Fidel said.

"Look, here comes dessert! Looks like Sacher Torte doesn't it? My, this was a good meal!"

"Just coffee for me," Fidel told the smiling waiter. "Annie, what would you say to combining some of our work? After you run your experiments, perhaps I can take the same subjects and run mine? Were you planning to have translators available?"

"Once we get to phase two? Definitely! It will add a good control to the experiments. Make sure they are responding with the semantic equivalents between languages."

"I know my subjects should be independently chosen, but I'm more interested first in finding out what the nexus does. I can always conduct a final experiment to be more fully random."

"I'm fine with it, as long as I get them first. I'm not planning on a confirmation trial, so I want them relatively untainted," Annie said and smiled impishly. She was feeling giddy with the prospect of working with the Insight 2500. She hadn't realized how much her current professional life represented a disappointment until presented with a means to achieve goals she hadn't dared to harbor.

After dinner, Fidel took the extra step of escorting her to the busy subway station. She wasn't sure whether there was more than a professional interest between them, but she was open to finding out. At a bare minimum, she would learn more about his specialties and perhaps find something there useful to her own projects. Getting a tan on vacation at Fidel's future beach house wouldn't be so bad either. She waved goodbye as she vanished into the maw of the subway station.

***

Six months later, she was set up in a lab space next to Fidel's in the Western Sensing building. It had taken almost an entire month to work out the details with the university. Her course load was lightened by the department assigning two graduate students who now took most of the lecture and section duties. They also graded papers and opened mail, much to Annie's delight. She was still expected to set and enforce the standard of instruction, which was easy enough given the help. Annie's agreement with Western Sensing was facilitated by their donation of renewable grants to fund the graduate students in her department. In short, all parties were happy. The university was pleased to participate in something they didn't have to fund; plus, the linguistics department hadn't delivered anything big in quite some time.

It took a little over a month on-site before Annie's routine was established enough to be familiar. Mornings were spent at the university, afternoons and evenings were spent at Western Sensing. Her first group of subjects presented themselves and Annie started to maximize the timeslots available on the Insight 2500 platform. The sessions would be completed there, and then a massive amount of data would be available for Annie to digest. At the end of the day, the time within the room-sized device was a mere fraction of the work time needed.

As Annie had said during the presentation, her first study was very simple. She acquired three groups of six subjects each: one group of native English speakers, one of native Spanish speakers, and one of native Chinese speakers. English and Spanish shared some portions of the same Latin roots, though English was more properly classified as a Germanic language. Chinese, though, was a completely separate branch. After being attuned to the Insight 2500, the subject would sit comfortably inside. Annie held up a common everyday item, such as a hairbrush or ball, and the subject identified the object aloud in their native tongue. Annie was halfway through the eighteen trials, when she had a bright idea. Why not tickle Fidel's neuron bundle herself and see what happened?

Subject 10, a native English speaker, was in the chair and had finished all of the identification tasks which Annie had teed up for him.

"Please sit for a couple of minutes while I adjust the scanner for the next portion," Annie called out as she worked the terminal console controlling the device. "It's ready, now I want you to tell me what happens, if anything, when I start? Are there any questions?"

Subject 10, who thought this experiment was the easiest $50 an undergraduate could make, said "Sure, no questions."

"OK, we're starting now," Annie said while watching the subject closely.

"Whoa! What's that? It's like I'm in a movie and I can't see you. What's wrong with my eyes? What the hell does that dog want?"

Annie terminated the excitation field and hurried to the test subject. He shook his head and then his eyes found Annie. "I can see normal again. That was crazy weird, what did you do? Is it some kind of image projector?"

"Why don't you describe what it was you saw," Annie pretended she wasn't shocked by the event.

"Ah, don't want to influence me? Right. OK, it was a weird room. It looked like a classic English manor library room, wood bookshelves, leather chairs, a fireplace with a painting over it. It even smelled of smoke and leather. There was a small table with brandy glasses and a snifter," Subject 10 said.

"You mentioned a dog?"

"Oh yeah, the dog. It was a white Labrador Retriever, but the size of a small pony. It looked at me as if it was saying something. It looked really smart."

"Are you sure it was white?"

"Yeah, it was. The room was more real than real life. Everything was more vivid, like 4K video, but in 3D!"

"You mentioned smell?"

"Yeah, I could smell the burning wood. Now that I remember, I could feel the waves of heat off of the fire, too. You know, like when you stand in front of a fireplace and can feel the heat even if you're not right next to it. Freaky! Is this testing a new entertainment system? If it is, sign me up!" Subject 10's enthusiasm was profound.

"One final question, I'm sorry to go back over it, but you say the dog was white?"

"Yes, white so white it blinded you to look into it. I know Labs aren't really white, but it looked like a white Lab. It seemed to want something, it just felt like that."

"That's all for today. When are you scheduled to work with Dr. Munos?" Annie asked.

"Tomorrow morning, bright and early."

"Thank you for your help, your check will be sent to the address provided."

"No, really what was the experiment all about?"

"I can't tell you until after the entire work is complete. You will get another chance at the last bit tomorrow morning, I'll tell you that much."

"Thanks, Dr. Richardson! Have a great evening!"

He sure seems happy, Annie thought. *Now I have to go tell Fidel I may have screwed up his pitch. Shit!*

Annie put the finishing touches on shutting down the lab and headed home for the evening dreading the impending conversation. Arriving too quickly, she put her key in the door, opening it to a warm greeting.

"Darling, you're early tonight! I'll reheat some dinner and get some wine while you relax," Fidel said as he rounded the kitchen countertop to kiss her soundly. Annie accepted the kiss and gave it back with interest before addressing the sober confession which had to be made.

"I have a confession, Love, and you might be angry with me," Annie started seriously.

Fidel pulled up two stools to the countertop and patted one. "Wait a second, end-of-day confessions require a glass of wine," and he was off to provide just that.

"I'm serious."

"OK, wine is still on the menu, in case I need it rather than just want it." Fidel poured two glasses and set them in front of their respective stools, plopping down on his own.

"Cheers, Love."

"I'm really sorry, Fidel, but I might have ruined one of your subjects for the study."

"What a relief! I thought you had found another lover and were leaving me! What happened?"

Annie related the entire set of events and sat waiting while Fidel mulled it over.

"I think I can use it, Annie. And it validates something I was beginning to worry about in my results. In fact, I was looking for someone discreet to replicate the work."

"What do you mean, what kind of results are you seeing?"

"I was beginning to think I was going crazy. In fact, if it wasn't for all the happy romance hormones I might have become seriously depressed. Here it is in a nutshell: everyone sees the dog. The same library, the same dog!"

"You're kidding!"

"No, I wish I was. No matter how I engage the neuron bundle the same result ensues. The Chinese speaker describes an English manor house library with many of the same features, including the knowing dog. The image appears to be movie-like, as the subject sees the room and can even look around for more details. The room persists solidly until I turn off the excitation. Then they can see normally. I would like to get some subjects who aren't culturally familiar with an English manor house, but it is almost impossible here."

"How widely spread, geographically, are the Insight 2500 demos being run?"

"Basically everywhere in the fifty largest economies. Why?" Fidel asked.

"Why don't we reach out to a researcher using the system, ask them to stimulate the neuron bundle, and see what comes back? Ask them to record the sessions on video as well as the built-in system. No foreshadowing of what we are expecting to hear. In the meantime, I think you better start writing your paper so you can publish first. You aren't angry with me?"

"Not a bit of it, and you're right; I have to be ready for publishing right away. Quick question before I delight you with leftovers, was your baseline neural data capture affected by the event?" Fidel asked.

"No, it wasn't. Oh, my!" Annie exclaimed in wonder.

"What?"

"I just thought of something I will have to look into. I would rather not say until I have something more solid. Do you mind if I run data similar to today's for the balance of my subjects?"

"Not at all, as long as you share that portion of the data-stream with me."

Annie reached out her hand and shook Fidel's, "Deal! Now, did someone mention food preparation?"

***

The next month was filled with activity, Annie kept her notions to herself though she was almost bursting with triumph. She had committed to not to share with Fidel until after the results came back from the three researchers overseas who had agreed to help. Fidel had most of his initial paper finished, and was engaged with the intellectual property lawyers for Western Sensing. The paper would announce the fact of the room's existence and how to invoke it. Once done, he would have precedence over other claimants, and subsequent papers could be more leisurely.

As results came back, Fidel feverishly collated the information, then asked Annie to come to his lab and see for herself.

"I'll just put the videos up on the screen. Our colleagues abroad subtitled their clips with English so we can understand what is being said." Fidel clicked to begin playback.

Annie settled into an office chair and watched the videos with amazement. As before, every subject saw a room, books, fire, and a large dog. Regardless of the mother tongue or culture, the semantic content was the same.

After the viewing, Fidel brought the lights back up. "Well, what do you think?"

"It is a wonderful thing, Fidel! You can be very proud. Publish immediately as the other researchers are now scrambling behind you, colleagues or not."

"The paper is ready for release, we were only waiting to see what came back from the others. We won't even wait for the journal's publication schedule. This one might go out on a press release as well. So, do you think Loci of Munos will be recognized?"

"Yes and no. It will be recognized, but I suspect the name will be something else entirely. Have you ever been to the British Museum, Love?"

"Yes, I saw all the marble and the Rosetta Stone. Great museum!"

"Do you remember what the Rosetta Stone enabled?"

"Wasn't it a piece of an Egyptian pharaoh's proclamation, but repeated in multiple tongues, the Greek version allowed us to understand the Egyptian text where before we could not?"

"Exactly. The consistency of your loci across multiple cultural and linguistic boundaries argues for it having a similar effect on our knowledge going forward. If I had to guess, I would say it will probably be called the Rosetta Loci."

"I don't understand."

"Think of it: the exact same scene linked to the semantic encoding of the room, but in many different tongues. With all of that information, the world is possible. A universal translator is the least of what it can do once fully researched. I can take that in combination with my work and determine finally how linguistic data is encoded within the brain. Someone else will doubtless devise a truth scanner. After all, if the semantic encoding is understood, a simple brain scan would tell the scanner everything about the subject. This changes everything!"

Fidel's face ran the gamut from a few seconds of excitement followed by a sudden look of dread, almost fear.

"What's the matter? I thought you would be excited and happy," Annie asked.

"I'm excited about what we can accomplish with the loci. My problem, which I just thought of, is something else entirely. As scientists, this discovery should frighten all of us to our very bones. I am."

"What? Why?" Annie reached out to comfort him.

Fidel turned his anguished face towards her, "Who put it in there, Annie? *What* put it in there?"

Annie opened her mouth to respond, and shut it without a sound. *Who indeed?*

BREAKFAST WITH HOWARD

"Is that you, Danny?" I heard as I entered the side door of my grandparents' house in the early morning.

"Yeah, it's me," I answered, thinking that if I were anyone else it would be too late to do anything about it.

"Come in the kitchen and pull up a chair."

I had walked the several blocks from our Bloomington, California home on Lynwood Street, crossing Valley Blvd and over to their home on Portola Avenue in the dark of the early morning. Mom always insisted I report to work early, so I generally got there well before Grandpa was ready to leave. That meant a second breakfast most days. Grandpa would be sitting at the kitchen table, smoking pretty much nonstop, and drinking black, percolated coffee. By the time I arrived, he was usually polishing off most of a can of biscuits and whatever bacon Grandma had prepared. Grandpa's biscuits of choice were the store-brand ones with 10 chunks of biscuit dough to a can; we could get them on sale at twelve cans for a dollar at the Safeway on Valley Blvd. The bacon could be any kind as long as it was pork.

During summer vacations and school year weekends of my early high school years, I had many opportunities to work for Howard Sharp, my maternal grandfather. At the time, I wouldn't have necessarily labeled them opportunities, but the improved vision one attains with age has since changed my mind.

My mother told me I had to help my grandfather. That was an argument I always fell for, as I dearly loved this particular grandfather. I made a little cash, but also learned house framing, drywall, painting, plumbing, piping, and landscaping. So yes, it was an opportunity.

Looking back, I can't imagine I was all that helpful. I had to be taught every task prior to being useful and Grandpa was still stronger than me when it was most needed, assuming he was wearing his trusty truss (as he jokingly referred to it). Most of what Grandpa did was manage and maintain his many rental properties as well as renovating new ones. So our tasks ranged from home construction to yard maintenance, depending on what was needed at the time.

Grandpa, like a vulture, was always on the lookout for single family homes that had been purchased under eminent domain and scheduled for demolition. He would swoop in, place a bid to remove the home, buying a framed house for pennies on the dollar. He'd lift the house frame up onto a trailer truck and move it to a vacant lot that he had previously prepared to receive it. Once placed, he reconnected and renovated the home then found a new tenant. The house I lived in was one of his better efforts.

Grandpa was always telling stories and cracking jokes while Grandma was always deadly serious. Grandpa was an adult friend and Grandma represented the forces of order and discipline.

"Have some biscuits and bacon. Odessa, cook up some more bacon for Danny," he flashed a mischievous grin and pointed out an empty chair at the stainless steel-trimmed dinette table.

Grandma greeted me, with a cloud of rose fragrance and as few hugs as I could reasonably manage, and then started cooking a whole new batch of bacon on the stove. She usually wore a lot of rose fragrance. The closer you got to her the more stifling it became. One had to hold their breath when getting a hug and kiss to avoid sneezing and coughing fits. Grandpa referred to it as her "chemical warfare." Truth told, she probably just didn't like the smell of cigarettes which permeated their home. The combination was enough to make me choke. Even adding bacon, biscuits and whatever else was being cooked to the mix wasn't sufficient to lift the curse.

Grandma was fairly short, close to five feet tall and built solid. We used to joke that she was probably five feet in circumference as well. She had a farmer's wife build: solid with large shoulders and legs like pillars, not a lot of jiggle. She usually dressed as though she was going to church: dress, fake pearls, girdle, rollup nylon stockings, and sensible dress shoes. The fake pearls came off when she was being casual.

Grandma was lacquered down, but never liquored up. Hair up and done all the time, held strictly in place by gallons of lacquer hairspray. The hairstyle was that of the Primitive Baptist Church in Texas where she grew up. As a younger child, my cousins and I would throw paper airplanes at her hair. Once, a particularly well-crafted effort crash-landed into her hair nose-first and stuck. Grandma went through her whole day not knowing why the grandkids were paralyzed with giggles. Grandpa saw it happen, shook his head, and smiled.

"Odessa doesn't need any more of these biscuits and bacon. One of these days, her girdle is going to burst and kill everyone in the room with shrapnel!" japed Grandpa.

Grandma waved her spatula at him half-threatening; he just laughed, coughed, and kept up the running dialog.

Grandpa wasn't much taller than Grandma, not overweight but solid as well. His daily uniform consisted of steel-toe work shoes, belted khaki pants, and a tucked-in single-pocket, short-sleeve cotton shirt. Grandpa's signal that he was ready for "bidness" was whenever he put his cigarettes in the shirt pocket. But generally that was sometime later in the morning.

Since Grandpa never left until the beginning of the normal workday, it left ample time for stories at the breakfast table. Later, I better understood he was treating his tenants respectfully by starting maintenance activities after their morning routines.

"Danny, did I ever tell you about the time I tangled with the croton oil?"

"Howard!" Grandma harrumphed, "That isn't a story for the breakfast table!"

Grandpa raised an eyebrow, grinned, and pulled on his cigarette.

I grinned back, waiting. I had heard this story many times before, but it was funny every time and I was not about to put a halt to it. Grandpa changed his stories just enough to make them new and interesting each time. He liked to tell stories about growing up in Oklahoma just prior to the Depression, but he also told dirty jokes once we got old enough to appreciate them. Of course, he didn't tell those jokes in front of Grandma, as that would have brought her over the counter! I told him our dirty jokes too, when alone. He always seemed to enjoy them, choking and coughing when he heard the punchlines. Sometimes, he would tell me a joke I had previously told him, only doing it better.

"You see, Danny, when I was a kid I used to steal our neighbor's watermelons," he began. "Actually, it was worse than stealing. We used to just crack them open and eat the hearts right there. We'd eat the heart, because that was the best part and it didn't have any seeds to slow you down, throw away the rest." He paused pulling on the cigarette. Grandpa had speaking rhythm I always associated with an Oklahoma accent. Later I would hear something very similar from Lakota Sioux storytellers. It added a cadence to the stories and was quite unusual for Southern California.

"Whether you're stealing watermelons or chickens, you gotta move fast! The farmers used to have rock-salt shotgun shells and were not reluctant to put a load into your backside if they caught you stealing. Well, the farmers weren't happy about losing their crops, so they used to leave traps for us. That was where the croton oil came in."

"What's croton oil, Grandpa?"

Grandpa chuckled. "Croton oil is a cattle laxative, for cattle that get constipated. A very powerful, fast-acting laxative. Danny, you'd think cattle, eating all that fiber like hay and grass, wouldn't get constipated. But they do, and they can die from it. You get constipated, you feel like you're dying, right? In a cow, all of that hay sometimes gets compressed into a plug which just won't move. One fix is to reach up into the cow's ass with your arm and try to stir things up by hand, breaking up or extracting the plug. That doesn't always work: you can break your arm and it definitely leaves you feeling dirty for a couple of weeks. Or you can just give 'em some croton oil. That takes care of bidness right directly. Makes a mess though."

"What was the farmer doing with the croton oil?" I asked.

"I was getting to that. You understand that a laxative powerful enough to work quickly on a cow is a darn sight stronger than Ex-Lax? Good! Anyhow, the farmers had a problem losing watermelons to local kids and they had a liquid laxative that is very strong. So what they do, Danny, is choose a couple of really big ripe watermelons still on the vine that are close to where we have been coming in to steal them at night. Roll them over a little, cut a core in the rind, pour some croton oil into the hole, put the plug back on the melon, setting it up so that you can't see the plug. Then leave it there for our night visits."

At this point, I was day-dreaming ways to get my hands on some croton oil and who I'd like to share it with, as he went on.

"So after dinner one night, I get a taste for some ripe watermelon. I make my excuses and fade away into the night over to that farmer's place. The coast looked clear, so I hopped the fence and looked for a good place to start.

In the moonlight, you can see pretty well, but you still have to thump 'em to check for ripe. I found a likely prospect, broke her open, scooped out the heart and ate the first one. Delicious, so I started looking for a second one, bend down to pick it up and then I couldn't stand up for the cramps. The flood gates opened up in the backside of my trousers and I thought I was dying right there. As much pain as I was in, I knew I couldn't make too much noise because of the farmer's shotgun and his dogs. So I stumble back to the road, collapsing in cramps every few feet, while that croton oil tried its best to reunite the watermelon heart with the field it came from."

As always at this point of the story, I was snorting with laughter in between bites of biscuit. So he moved in for the kill.

"If that farmer had wanted to, he could have tracked me home next day. I left a pretty clear trail!"

He tucked the pack of cigarettes into his shirt pocket, "Time to get to work, Danny. We can't sit around here like Odessa, eating biscuits and bacon all day."

And off we went to meet the demands of the day.

www.ingramcontent.com/pod-product-compliance
Lightning Source LLC
Chambersburg PA
CBHW021140190726
48288CB00008B/2753